The Dark City

The Guardians of Elestra #1

Thom Jones

Peekaboo Pepper Books

DEDICATION

This book was inspired by my sons, Galen and Aidan who listened to the stories and gave me great ideas along the way, reminding me that childhood is magical and funny. The book would never have made it to its final form without the editing of my wife Linda. Finally, I dedicate my continued work on this series to little Dinara who will soon be old enough to hear these stories.

The Dark City, Guardians of Elestra #1

Also available in the Guardians of
Elestra series:

To learn more about Elestra, including maps,
history, Tobungus' blog, Glabber's menu, and
contests that allow readers to submit ideas
for new characters, places, or other magical
things, please visit:

www.guardiansofelestra.com

CONTENTS

The Prophecy of the Twin Flames

A cold wind blew across the land.
A curtain of darkness followed.
Years passed, and hope for the light dwindled.
Finally, out of the darkness, two tiny flames emerged.
The fires burned, through battles great and small.
The flames grew to challenge the darkness itself. . .

1 The Weeping Moon

Derek Hughes and his twin sister Deanna decided to stay up a little later than their mother usually allowed. After all, it was summer, so there would be no school the next day. They had turned the light out in their room to fool their parents and sat next to the open window to make their plans in the moonlight. They thought and thought, and then thought some more, but came up with nothing. The room was dark, so they couldn't play a game or read. They both loved riddles, but neither of them could think of any.

They were just about to give up and go to sleep when they heard a strange noise outside. They leaned closer to the window and heard a soft weeping sound carried along on the wind. They looked at each other and wondered who could be in their backyard weeping.

They squinted as they tried to catch a glimpse of the unknown person hiding in the shadows, but saw no one. The sound grew steadily louder. It seemed to be coming at them from all sides. After nearly five minutes of searching the darkness, they saw a thin figure walking toward the back of their yard. "That's Grandpa," Derek whispered.

"What's he doing outside tonight?" Deanna replied. "Do you think he's the one who's weeping?"

"I hope not," Derek said. "He could be trying to figure out what's going on."

They ducked down so that their eyes barely peeked above the window sill and watched their grandfather moving slowly toward the old lantern post near the back of the yard. The lantern post was just a wooden post stuck in the ground with an old-fashioned lantern perched on top. They never paid much attention to the post, except when they used it as a base in games of tag. Their grandfather got to the post and reached up with both hands. He gripped the glass and metal lantern tightly and struggled to turn it. With a haunting creek that cut through the eerie weeping, the lantern twisted a quarter turn.

Derek and Deanna looked at each other again, still wondering what was happening. They turned back to their grandfather who bent down slightly and seemed to be looking at the lantern from below. Suddenly, the old man began to glow bright red. Seconds later, there was nothing but a huge ball of light that swirled around the post and whooshed into the lantern.

"Grandpa!" they both yelled frantically, but when the light faded, they saw that he really was gone.

Before they could think of what they should do, the bedroom door burst open. They gasped in surprise at the sound behind them. Their father was standing in the doorway, squinting to see where they were. He turned on the light and asked, "Why aren't you two in bed yet?"

"Dad," Derek began, "we just saw Grandpa out back. He went to the old lantern post, and um, I'm not really sure what he did." Looking at Deanna, he said, "Tell Dad what Grandpa did with the red light."

"Well, I know this sounds weird," Deanna said. "Grandpa sort of bent down by the old lantern, and then he disappeared in a cloud of red light."

"Red," their father whispered. Then, he coughed as if he had not said anything. "It's late. I'm sure you were dreaming." Before they could argue, he said, "Listen, kids, I have to get up really early to go on a business trip tomorrow, so please get to sleep."

Deanna straightened up to say something, but her father held up his hand. "I mean it. It's bedtime. There's nothing to worry about." He turned out the light and closed their door as he left.

The children waited a few seconds before sneaking to the door and quietly turning the knob. As the door opened, they could hear their parents' voices down the hall. "What do you have to do?" their mother asked.

"I have to go to the High Council," their father answered. "It's the Night of the Moonsign and my dad's gone off on his own. His stone will be free tomorrow when the sun rises. He was supposed to wait for me, but I don't think he wanted me to go before my time. I'll do what I can, but you'd better call your sisters and see if someone can watch the kids. It looks like the prophecy we feared is coming true."

"Can't we stop them?" their mother said in a worried voice.

"Ariel, we've always known that they would go," their father said. "The Seers of the Seventh Realm have seen their journey. We cannot undo a future that is certain."

"I just wish we could go with them to protect them," she whispered.

"My dear, it won't be long before they will protect us and many others," their father said. "I don't suppose you could convince your brother to help watch them," he said half jokingly.

Their mother shook her head, looking angry. "No, he chose his own path a long time ago. He wants to live his simple life on his farm and let the world pass by." The voices died down as their parents walked downstairs. Moments later, they heard their father's car pulling out of the driveway.

"What do you think that all meant?" Derek asked Deanna in a hushed voice.

"I think it means we're not dreaming," replied Deanna grimly. "I also think we should go out back and see if we can find Grandpa."

"You're right," Derek said. "I'll get our flashlights." He got the flashlights from the large bookshelves along the far wall and put them in their backpacks.

They kept all sorts of things in their backpacks for their hikes in the nearby woods. They had a compass, water bottles, whistles, books about insects and reptiles, a magnifying glass, and candy bars.

They were about to leave the room when Deanna whispered, "Wait." She walked over to her dresser and opened a small silver jewelry box that was sitting on top. From it, she pulled a braided headband decorated with silver moon-shaped beads.

In the darkness, the headband seemed to glow with its own inner light. Deanna slid the headband into her long brown hair. Derek saw what she was doing and grabbed a rope wristband interlaced with moon-shaped granite stones from a bookcase in the corner. He wrapped the wristband around his left wrist.

Their grandfather had given them the headband and wristband three weeks earlier on their eleventh birthday and told the children to wear them when they went on adventures. Even though the lantern post was just in the backyard, it still seemed like they were going on an adventure.

They silently crept out of their room, down the back stairs, and into the backyard. When they got to the lantern post, they saw no sign of their grandfather.

The soft weeping still floated on the wind. The grass under their feet was wet with dew, and there was a slightly sweet smell in the air. Derek bent down and looked at the bottom of the lantern, but saw nothing.

"I don't get it," he said, "what was Grandpa looking for?"

Deanna was standing behind Derek, watching him as he looked at the lantern. She bent down to see if she could see anything. As she did, the weeping grew a little louder. She stood back up and the sound faded. She looked to the right of the lantern and saw the full moon. She looked back at the lantern, then at the moon again, as if she was trying to figure out a puzzle in her mind.

Derek turned around and asked what she was doing. Without answering, she pushed past him and grabbed the lantern. She turned it a few inches so that it lined up with the moon.

"Alright," she said, "let's look at the moon through the lantern together. I think that's what Grandpa did."

Deanna grabbed Derek's shirt sleeve and bent down to look at the moon through the yellowish glass of the lantern. Derek pushed his hair away from his eyes, wanting to be sure that he saw every possible detail. As they crouched down, the weeping grew even louder. They looked at each other and then at the moon.

Suddenly, they felt a warm wind whip their cheeks. They stood as still as statues as a brilliant blue light surrounded them. In an instant, they were gone, and the blue light shot into the lantern.

On a winding dirt road on the hill overlooking their house, their father stood next to his car. He was watching the backyard and saw the ball of blue light disappear into the lantern. "Good luck, my beautiful children," he whispered before getting back into the car and driving into the night.

2 The Cave Prison

Derek and Deanna felt like they were spinning a thousand miles an hour with blue streaks of lightning flashing around them. They realized that they were floating because they could wiggle their feet without losing their balance.

Very slowly, the light faded and their feet hit solid ground. They squinted, trying to see what had happened. When the blue light had completely disappeared, they were surrounded by total darkness. There was no sound other than their breathing. "Derek?" Deanna whispered.

"Yeah, I'm here," he said, trying to sound brave. "I'll get my flashlight."

He dug around in his backpack and finally grabbed the cold metal tube. He clicked the switch and stepped back in surprise. They were standing in a passageway made of stone. He looked down and saw that the floor was stone too, with a thick covering of dust.

Deanna fished her flashlight out of her backpack and turned it on. They studied the walls, floors, and ceiling, but saw nothing but rock. The hallway, or whatever it was, went straight into the darkness for twenty feet or so before curving sharply to the right.

"Grandpa," Deanna called hesitantly. Suddenly, a cold wind rushed past them. Deanna felt like something was telling her to be quiet.

"Come on," Derek whispered and headed toward the curve in the hallway. He saw that Deanna looked nervous, so he said, "Listen, we have to find a way out of here, and unless you have a rock hammer, we need to look for a door."

Deanna made a face at Derek. He knew that she had a rock hammer that she used to open geodes to find the crystals inside, but she had left it in the bedroom. Besides, she couldn't break through a rock wall with a little hammer. She nodded, took a deep breath, and walked carefully into the darkness.

The hallway curved to the right, and then to the left. After nearly ten minutes of walking along the winding path, they saw the beams of their flashlights reflect off of something at the edges of the flashlights' reach. As they approached the object, they were confused by what they saw.

At first, they thought that it was a large glass tube with a statue inside. The statue was of a very old man who had a long beard. His face and hands were white like marble, but his beard looked almost real. He also looked different from other statues that they had seen at museums or parks, because he looked scared, or maybe confused. He was alone in the tube, except for a slowly swirling cloud of fog, which covered him from his chest to his feet.

Deanna shined her flashlight near the bottom of the tube and saw a golden plate with flowing writing. *"Baladorn, the Mighty,"* she read aloud. "He must have been some sort of king," she whispered.

Just then, another gust of cold wind swept past them. She looked at Derek, but saw that he was staring further down the path. He started to take a few steps when she reached out to stop him.

"Deanna, there's another tube up ahead," he said with excitement shining in his determined eyes. He walked quickly to the next tube and saw a second statue. This one looked a bit younger and shorter. The golden plate said, *"Mindoro, the Slightly Less Mighty."* Derek chuckled at the odd name and looked at Deanna, who still seemed scared, but also let out a little laugh.

"What do you think this place is?" Deanna asked. "Who would put statues in these glass tubes and then put the tubes in a pitch black cave? Why bother to name the statues and write the names on fancy gold signs?"

"I don't know, Deanna, the Slightly Less Tall," he said laughing. Even though they were both tall for their age, Derek had always been an inch taller than Deanna and loved to tease her about it.

"Ha, ha, Derek, the Scared of Worms," she replied, laughing even harder.

"Very funny. I was four when that happened." He knew that Deanna would always tease him about how he freaked out after falling down in the garden and getting covered by worms. "Look, let's just keep going."

They both looked down the hall and saw yet another tube. The third tube announced that the statue was of *Gelladrell, the Mightier Than Most*. They looked at each other and wondered about the odd names. They kept walking and found *Pontifree, the Short and Happy*; *Barndoble, the Smiling*; *Rentukis, the Weird*; *Felborn, the Hairy*; *Wipsaw, the Quirky*; *Dibbolotus, the Messy*; *Zirkat, the Itchy and Nervous*; *Nemnom, the Loud and Hungry*; and *Robretus, the Strangely Orange*.

They had found twelve tubes with statues and were having so much fun reading the odd names that they had forgotten their fear. When they got to the thirteenth tube, they immediately looked at the golden plate, without looking at the statue. The plate read *"Phillipe, the Brave."* Before they could say anything, they saw the statue move slightly. They looked up and saw their grandfather inside the tube. He was ash white like the other statues, but he was moving very slowly.

"Grandpa," Deanna said frantically, "what's wrong with you?"

Their grandfather opened his mouth and whispered, "Don't worry about me, children." The words seemed to struggle to escape from the old man's lips.

"What do you mean?" Deanna cried. "You look like a ghost."

"I'll be fine," the old man mumbled. "You have to worry about yourselves." He paused to catch his breath in the slowly rising fog. "You are the final generation. You have to stop the Dark Wizard Eldrack. If he holds the keys to all fifteen moon gates, he will merge the worlds of Elestra and rule over all creatures."

Derek felt all over the tube trying to find a way to open it. He was more interested in getting his grandfather out than in hearing some story about a wizard. "How can we get you out?" he called.

"You can't free me," their grandfather murmured. "Not yet. If you try to release me, Eldrack will know it, and he will send his armies. You are the only ones who have entered the Cave of Imprisonment without being captured. We knew you'd follow me, but he didn't know you were coming. Now, you must take a journey through Elestra and retrieve the fifteen sacred moonstones."

Derek was still fiddling with the tube. "Derek," their grandfather said calmly, "you came through the lantern. You know in your heart that you can't save me . . . not now."

Derek took a step back from the tube. "What's Elestra, and what are moonstones?" he asked in a shaky voice.

"Elestra is a world where six magical kingdoms exist in harmony," their grandfather said. "The moonstones you will seek are spread throughout these kingdoms. Above Elestra, there are fifteen moons. Each moon is a magical gateway to one of the outworlds which are totally separate from each other."

He took a slow breath and continued, "The people on some of the outworlds, such as our world, don't even know that they are connected to Elestra. King Barado, a wizard from one of the outworlds, protects Elestra and the Moongates that lead to the outworlds. Eldrack is an evil wizard who has spent hundreds of years preparing to conquer Elestra and gain enough power to break through the Moongates. Our world is one that he will seek to capture. Eldrack needs to expand his magic to win the battle against Barado. There are three ways that Eldrack can increase his magical powers and control Elestra. First, he can find all fifteen moonstones and use them to absorb the magic of each world."

"How would he do that?" Deanna asked.

"The moonstones are magical lenses that concentrate the power of the outworlds. When a wizard looks through a moonstone at the moon it belongs to, he will gain the magical power of that world. This can only be done by a wizard who already has great magical powers. For anyone else, the moonstone is nothing more than a piece of colored glass. Not even King Barado holds the power over the Moongates." He paused to take a slow, shallow breath.

"The second way for Eldrack to increase his magical power is to capture fifteen generations of Mystical Guardians and steal their power." He looked deep into the children's eyes and said, "We are a family of wizards who help to protect Elestra from Eldrack and the Dark Wizards who have come before him. But, Eldrack has discovered our secret and captured thirteen generations of our family. Two more generations, and he will have the power to defeat King Barado. If he has our family and the moonstones, his power will be unstoppable."

"Then we have to get you out," Deanna said, "so that you can stop him."

"No, I am too weak from my capture. I should not have come alone. I'm afraid that I have only enough strength for one more spell."

He raised his hand, and they saw that he was holding a craggy branch which he touched to the inside of the glass tube. He muttered a few words which they could not understand, and the tip of the branch glowed a brilliant green. The branch moved through the glass and fell to the ground. When Deanna reached down to pick it up, she saw that a necklace with a silver charm was wrapped around it.

"That is the Wand of Ondarell," their grandfather said. "It is one half of the most powerful set of wands ever created. They were forged in the pit of the Kutama Volcano. After you have located all of the moonstones, you will be able to locate the other wand. When the two halves are used together, they will hold enough power to defeat any magical army."

He breathed heavily. "The necklace has the Book of Spells in the charm. You can use the spells from the book with the wand to help you along your way."

Before he could go on, Deanna opened the tiny silver charm that was shaped like a book. Suddenly, a huge brown book burst from the charm. The book had a tattered cover with pictures of dragons and other creatures which she had never seen. She looked at the book for a few seconds and then closed the charm which made the book disappear. She turned her head toward Derek and smiled slightly.

Derek looked like he was thinking through what their grandfather had told them. "Wait a second, Grandpa. You said that there were three ways that Eldrack could gain power."

"Yes, that is correct," the old man said. "The third way would involve an attack on the Magical Wells in Elestra, but that would require a huge magical army, and Eldrack would only do that when he was really ready to start his final move against the king."

Derek looked at their grandfather and said, "Are you sure we can't get you out of here?"

"Yes, I'm tired," he replied. "I need to rest and regain my strength. I was able to put a spell on the inside of this tube. I will not fall completely under Eldrack's power."

He looked at them intently. "Derek. Deanna. You were not supposed to learn about our family's secret until you were fourteen, but now you must do what those before you have failed to do. You have a great adventure in front of you. You will see wondrous things, fight great battles, and face powerful enemies. You hold the key to saving Elestra. When you leave this cave, you will see the Dark City of Amemnop. There, you will find the first moonstone, and you will also find friends to help you on your way." He took a slow, shallow breath and gathered the strength to say one last thing before falling into a magical sleep. "Now, go before Eldrack returns."

Derek and Deanna touched the glass that imprisoned their grandfather and said a final goodbye. Then, they hurried further down the path until they came to an exit which led them into the cool Elestra night. They looked out over a valley at the most amazing sight they had ever seen.

Overhead, there were fifteen moons shining brightly on the land below. The thick forests, glimmering lakes, and rushing rivers were all lit up in the glowing night. The only dark area was a city which sat below the cave, past a thick forest.

"Amemnop," Deanna said, as she squeezed the Wand of Ondarell.

"The Dark City," Derek added.

Derek and Deanna started down the path to their first adventure in Elestra.

3 The Riddle of the Dew Drop Forest

Deanna and Derek followed a worn path, brightly lit by the moonlight. Derek held his flashlight and Deanna clutched the Wand of Ondarell tightly. The path was surrounded by knee-high grasses, so they were confident that nothing was waiting in the shadows to jump out at them. After twenty minutes of walking under Elestra's fifteen moons, they saw the shadowy edges of a forest in front of them.

"Well," Deanna said nervously, "the Dark City is on the other side of the forest, so I guess we have to go through."

Derek was hoping that the light of Elestra's moons would show them the way through the forest, but he turned on his flashlight just to make sure that it would work if they needed it. When they passed the first trees, they found that the path opened into a wide circle, with six paths going off into different parts of the forest. They looked at each other, not knowing which way to go.

Deanna was about to suggest the middle path, which seemed to go straight into the forest, when a squeaky voice said, "Can't decide which path to choose? Yes. Yes. So many others have wandered the forest for years without ever finding their way out."

Derek and Deanna looked around but saw no one. "Who's there?" asked Derek. "Who said that?"

"It was I," the same squeaky voice said.

Deanna looked down and saw a huge frog on the forest floor. "You?" she said. "You're a . . . a frog."

"A+, young lady, you know what a frog is," the frog replied, "but do you know what type of frog I am?"

"As big as you are, I'd say you're a bullfrog," Derek answered.

"A what?" the frog sputtered indignantly. "Junior, do I look like a bull?"

"Junior?" Derek said in surprise. "Look here froggy! I didn't say bull. I said *bullfrog*."

"Derek!" Deanna snapped. "Be nice."

Derek looked back and forth between Deanna and the frog, not knowing if he should continue the argument or settle down and see if the frog could help them.

"Well, Sonny," the frog went on, "you need a class on frogs. I don't moo, and I don't chew cud. I'm a wood frog." The frog quickly jumped against one of the huge trees and transformed into a miniature man, no more than two feet tall.

"How did you do that?" Deanna asked.

"So full of questions," the man replied. "Is that really the most important question you have for me?"

Deanna thought for a few seconds and said, "Okay, here's a better question. Which path should we choose to get through the forest to the Dark City?"

"Ah, you wish to go to Amemnop. Very well, but first, I must ask you a question. Do you serve King Barado or the Dark Wizard Eldrack?"

Derek spoke first. "We serve neither. We come in the name of the Mystical Guardians, and we must enter the Dark City as quickly as possible."

"Mystical Guardians, eh? Well, Eldrack won't be pleased to hear that." He laughed heartily. "Good, let him be upset. Now, about the path. I can't tell you which path to choose.

Derek sighed loudly, thinking that the frog was still mad at him for calling him a bullfrog.

"Relax," the little man said, "I can give you the riddle that will guide you if you are clever enough. You are in luck because it is night. The riddle is really quite simple."

He took a step closer to them and instantly turned back into a frog. He jumped against another tree and turned back into a man. It was obvious that he only turned into a man when he jumped against one of the towering trees. The children realized that every step he took turned him back into a frog, so he probably had to stay near the trees in the forest if he wanted to turn into a man.

"What's the riddle?" Deanna asked impatiently.

The frog croaked loudly, as if to say "settle down." He took a slow breath and burped an uneven *ribbit* before reciting the riddle. "*Alone, you cannot escape from the forest. Only with the help of the visitors of the night can you find your way through.*"

"The visitors of the night," Derek repeated. "Maybe it's some type of animal or insect that moves through the forest at night." They looked around for over ten minutes without finding any sort of living creature other than the frog. "What visits the forest at night?" Derek asked desperately.

The little man stood watching them. He kept muttering, "Bullfrog? How can he confuse me with a bull. Maybe he needs glasses."

Derek pushed a vine aside to see if anything was hiding under a particularly large tree. A huge leaf rattled and a few drops of water splashed down on Derek and Deanna who looked up in surprise.

"Is it starting to rain?" Deanna asked. She looked up through the trees and saw the moons shining in a cloudless sky and realized that it was not raining. "Where did that water come from?" she asked.

Derek looked at a nearby leaf and said, "It's dew. The leaves are covered with it." His face lit up as he realized that dew comes at night. "Deanna, dew is the night visitor."

Suddenly, their grandfather's words came to her. "You can use the spells from the book with the wand to help you on your way." Deanna took the silver charm from around her neck and opened the Book of Spells.

Derek held the flashlight on the book, while she quickly leafed through the pages until she found what she was looking for. In the pale moonlight, she read aloud:

From the Great Waterfalls of the Antuga Highlands, the Waters of Elestra come at night as Dew Drops. Now Dew Drops, hear the call of Ondarell and guide us through the great forest so that we may enter the gates of Amemnop.

The tip of the wand glowed for a second and then went dark.

"Look, Deanna," Derek said, pointing to a leaf on the far side of the circle.

In the semi-darkness, they could see tiny circles of light covering the surface of the leaf. When they got closer, they realized that the dew drops on the leaf had begun to glow in the damp night. They saw that three more leaves, leading down one of the paths were also covered in glowing dew drops. At first, they walked down the dew-lit path, but after a while, they began running along the route to Amemnop.

As they ran, Deanna heard a rustling sound behind them. She looked back and saw the frog-man struggling to keep up with them. With every step, he transformed from man to frog, so he had to keep jumping against the trees to turn back into a man. The extra jumps made his journey harder than theirs, and he fell further behind.

"Hold on," Deanna said to Derek. She pointed back to the frog and said, "I think he wants to travel along with us."

They slowed down to a jog and finally saw the edge of the tree line. When they came to the end of the forest path, they stopped to speak with the little man again. "We never got your name," Deanna said.

He took several deep breaths to stop his panting and said, "I am Aramaltus, Forest Keeper of King Barado."

"It's good to hear that you serve King Barado," Derek said. "We don't know who to trust in Elestra yet."

"Most creatures from Elestra support King Barado," Aramaltus began, "but there are a few who follow Eldrack. He pays the Gong Beaters of the Floddan Lowlands to follow him. They're really an irritating bunch. They do nothing but beat their gongs all day. I think he wants them to irritate everyone else in Elestra. There are also some creatures from the outer moon worlds which have come to Elestra with Eldrack to gain more power."

"Were you serious that some people wander through the forest for years?" Derek asked.

"Oh, yes. There are even villages deep in the forest where lost travelers have decided to live."

"What can you tell us about Amemnop?" Deanna asked hopefully.

"I know very little of the Dark City of Amemnop," Aramaltus said. "I cannot leave the forest, so I only hear bits and pieces about the city. The only thing I remember is that an old man came through the forest and said that Amemnop will remain dark as long as the Fountain of the Six Kingdoms remains quiet."

"What are the Six Kingdoms?" Derek asked.

"I have been in this forest for so long that I am not really the best person to ask about the six kingdoms. When I was a child, I recall my parents telling me stories about dragons and snow-white kangaroos, ice warriors and rock creatures, and many other strange beings. But that was so long ago that I scarcely remember," Aramaltus replied. "I guess that you and your Mystical Guardian friends have your first mystery."

"We don't have any friends," Deanna said. "It's just us."

"Just you? But you're kids."

"That's right, Aramaltus," Derek said, "but we have to search for the moonstones before Eldrack finds them."

"In that case," Aramaltus replied as he reached down to the ground, "take this mushroom with you." He handed a large brown mushroom with red markings to Deanna. "When you need assistance, knock on the top of the mushroom, as you would a door." Before Deanna could ask him about the mushroom, Aramaltus jumped away into the forest.

Deanna put the mushroom into her backpack and headed with Derek toward the gated entrance to Amemnop.

4 Tobungus The Fungus among Us

Deanna reached the Gate to Amemnop first and eagerly walked through it. Derek was beginning to think that he needed a turn with the wand. His flashlight seemed pretty weak in comparison. He would wait to mention this to Deanna because she seemed so confident with the wand, and he didn't know what dangers they would face in the Dark City. He pushed through the wooden gate and saw a town that looked like an old-west ghost town from books he had read. The streets were dusty, the buildings were worn, and everything was dark.

"Where should we look first?" Deanna asked quietly.

"How should I know?" Derek snapped back. The creepy stillness of the city was making him feel nervous. "I'm sorry, Deanna," he said, "I didn't mean to yell at you."

"I know," she said. She looked around, but saw no one on the streets. "I think this entire town is abandoned." They moved to the sidewalk which they found was made of wood planks. The only sounds they heard were their own footsteps on the creaking wood.

"It sure seems empty." He pulled out his flashlight and clicked the switch. Nothing happened. He looked at the flashlight and saw that the light bulb was lit, but the light stopped at the glass. "Deanna?" he said uncertainly.

Deanna looked over and saw that the flashlight looked like it had a frozen beam of light struggling to escape the bulb. Derek pointed the flashlight straight up and looked down into it. The beam of light shot up and nearly blinded him. "What did you do?" Deanna asked.

"I don't know," he replied. He tilted the flashlight back down and the light went dead. "I don't get it," he said. He kept moving the flashlight around and it remained dark, except when he pointed it straight up.

"Do you get the idea that there's some magic spell working on your flashlight?" Deanna asked.

"That's what I was thinking," Derek said. "Maybe you can use a spell from the book to fix it."

Deanna opened the charm and the book appeared, but it was too dark to read any of the spells, so she closed the book again. "Wait a minute," she said. She reached into her backpack and pulled out the mushroom that Aramaltus had given them. "Here goes." She gently knocked on the top of the mushroom.

The mushroom shot from her hand and began to spin like a mini-tornado. As it spun, it grew until it was nearly four feet tall. It stopped spinning, and Derek and Deanna took a step closer to it. They were shocked when a pair of eyes just below the mushroom's cap opened. "Whoo," the mushroom said. The mushroom had a face and arms and legs which popped out from its thick stem.

"What in the world?" Deanna asked.

"Hold on," the mushroom said. He reached his arm around and fished out a pair of shoes from a bag which seemed to appear from nowhere. He put the shoes on and began to dance on the wooden planks. "I'm free," he yelled.

"Shh," Deanna whispered, holding her hands out.

Derek looked down at the mushroom's feet. "You've got to be kidding," he said, not believing what he was seeing. "A tap-dancing mushroom?"

"Yes, yes, I see," the mushroom said, "Tap shoes are too festive. This is a dark and dreary place. Perhaps something a bit quieter. No, wait, I know." He took the tap shoes off and put on a pair of cowboy boots.

"I'm dreaming," Derek said.

"Dreaming? That's an odd name," the mushroom said. "Well, I'm Tobungus."

"Tobungus, the. . . " Deanna started.

"That's right, Tobungus the Fungus," the mushroom replied, bowing to the twins.

"Excuse me," Derek said, "my name's Derek, not dreaming. And this is my sister Deanna."

"It's nice to meet you, but I have to warn you that I'm terrible with names. Don't be mad if I call you something else. In fact, I've forgotten already. Wait, let me guess. Hairball and Stinky?"

"Derek and Deanna," Derek corrected.

"Wow, I don't know where I got the hairball thing. Well, maybe I do. The last people I traveled with had a cat. Miserable long-haired beast that coughed all over. Don't get me wrong. I usually love cats. But, that little monster tried to scratch me every chance it got. I'll get your names right eventually."

"Where did you get all the shoes?" Deanna asked.

"From my shoe bag," Tobungus replied. He saw that Deanna looked confused. "All mushrooms have two bags. The bigger bag is filled with all of our shoes. Surely you knew that."

"Yeah, right, surely," Derek muttered. "What about the other bag?"

Tobungus pulled out the second bag and dumped it on the ground. "Let's see. This has all of my really important stuff — raincoat, butter, ruler, marbles, notebook, a cup, a kazoo, my bagpipes, and, of course, my magic lemon."

"How did you fit bagpipes into that bag?" Derek asked. "It's only about the size of a backpack."

"It's a minimizing bag," Tobungus answered. "Everything I put in shrinks to fit the bag."

As Tobungus was gathering up his things, Deanna said, "Look, Tobungus, my brother and I just came to Elestra a couple of hours ago. This is all new to us, so we'll need your help. We are Mystical Guardians, from the family of Baladorn. All of our relatives here have been captured by Eldrack, and he'll try to get us next. We have a very important mission to complete, and it starts right here, in this town. Do you know anything about Amemnop that might help us?"

Tobungus nodded as if he was used to unusual occurrences in Elestra. He didn't seem surprised to find himself in the company of these young Guardians on their quest "Well, it's been a while since I've been here." He stopped and tilted his head at an odd angle. "I've only been here a few times since Eldrack cast his spell on the city."

"What kind of spell did he use?" Deanna asked hopefully.

"He created a Shield of Darkness which blocks any light within the city, except light shining straight upward," Tobungus replied. "Without light, the city has shriveled up like a dying plant. Everything in the city had life when the magic flowed. Now, there is almost no magic, so it's like the buildings are gasping for breath. Look around. No one walks the streets anymore."

"I don't suppose you know how to break the spell," Derek said.

"Not a clue! But," he was thinking hard, "there was a little diner around here somewhere. It was owned by an old man who had once been the City's ParaMage. No, wait, I'm wrong. He didn't own it. He was the cook."

"What's a ParaMage?" Deanna asked hopefully.

"A ParaMage is like the city's magical leader. He protects the city from dark wizards and oversees all magical places in the city. Being the ParaMage of Amemnop is a pretty big deal."

"He sounds like someone we should talk to," Deanna said.

Tobungus was already walking quickly along the wooden sidewalk. He finally stopped in front of a dark building with boarded-up windows. "If this was the diner, it looks like it went out of business," she said.

There was no sign with the diner's name, and every window had been covered. Derek still had his barely glowing flashlight in his hand, and Tobungus reached out and pointed it up at the overhang. The light from the flashlight shot upward and lit up a sign attached to the ceiling over the walkway. The sign read *Glabber's Grub Hut*.

"Here we are," Tobungus said. He pushed open the door and the kids heard the voices of dozens of people inside.

5 Butter and Magic

Tobungus walked into Glabber's Grub Hut, but Derek and Deanna stopped outside to talk for a second before going in. "He seems kind of weird," Deanna said.

"You're not kidding," Derek said. "He carries butter around with him, not to mention the bag of shoes."

"Yes, but Aramaltus gave him to us, so he must trust him," Deanna said.

"But, then again," Derek added, "Aramaltus is a frog with a short temper."

They looked at each other, not sure what they should think. They finally took a deep breath and walked into the diner. They saw Tobungus moving toward the counter near the back of the building. The inside of the diner was brightly lit, and the room was filled with people sitting around tables mounded with foods of all types.

"Glabber," Tobungus called out.

"Tobu," came the reply from a huge snake that was coiled up on the counter. "It's been a long time."

"Yes, my old friend," Tobungus said, "I need to speak with Iszarre-Ham." He looked around nervously, pointed at Derek and Deanna, and whispered, "My friends Dreamy and Dinky need to see him also."

Before Deanna could correct him about their names, the snake said, "Iszarre's rather busy, with the lunch crowd coming soon. What do you have to offer?"

Tobungus reached into his bag and pulled out a stick of butter and waved it in the air in front of the snake. "Is that what I think it is?" Glabber asked.

"Yep, it's pure butter," Tobungus said. "You can have the whole thing if we can see Iszarre-Ham."

Glabber waved them toward a door behind the counter with his tail and then started to chew on the solid stick of butter that Tobungus set on the counter.

Tobungus called, "Flipper and Chop, hurry up!"

"Are you Flipper, or am I?" Derek kidded Deanna.

Tobungus turned and whispered to the kids, "Butter is like gold here in Elestra." He opened the door and they found themselves in a steamy, messy kitchen. A very old man was hunched over a griddle cooking something that looked like pancakes. He looked up and saw them watching him. He straightened up and turned away from the griddle. "Can I help you?" he asked in a tired voice.

"Are you Iszarre-Ham?" Derek asked, wondering how someone so old and so tired could possibly help them on their journey.

The old man laughed, and his purple eyes twinkled, giving Derek the impression that there was more to this cook than he was letting them see.

"My name is Iszarre, but here in Elestra, wizards are given the title Ham out of respect. It's a little embarrassing, so please just call me Iszarre." Derek nodded that he understood. "Can I help you?" he repeated.

"I hope so," Deanna began. "We're searching for a moonstone, but we don't know where to look."

"Moonstone? Why would two children be looking for a moonstone in Amemnop?" The old man's voice seemed more awake, but he was trying to hide his interest.

"Because if we don't find it, Eldrack will soon have enough power to defeat King Barado," Derek said. The old man looked more interested. "Because, we are the final generation of Mystical Guardians," Derek added.

"You are Mystical Guardians," Iszarre said in disbelief. "How old are you?"

"We're eleven," Deanna said, "almost twelve."

"So, you've learned that you are Mystical Guardians before you have turned fourteen," Iszarre said.

"That's right," Deanna said. "Of course, we only found out tonight. We were told to start our quest for the moonstones in Amemnop. We heard a story that the city was put under a spell and will remain dark as long as the Fountain of the Six Kingdoms remains quiet."

"Aramaltus must have told you that." Deanna nodded, and Iszarre continued, "Yes, I told him that several years ago. I heard Baladorn say that before he disappeared." Looking down, he said, "That was a dark time for Elestra." Straightening up again, he added, "But, I don't know where the moonstone is."

"Baladorn?" Derek said. "We saw Baladorn frozen in the Cave of Imprisonment."

"So, it's true," Iszarre said. "Baladorn has been captured by Eldrack." He continued to flip the pancakes, lost in thought.

Finally, he sighed, "I'm not sure what he meant about the fountain remaining quiet, but I can tell you a bit about the fountain. The Six Kingdoms, or Realms, are the Icelands, the Sky Dragons, Oceania, the Forest Kingdom, the Desert Realm, and Magia. Deep in the past, the leaders of the Six Kingdoms decided that Amemnop would be the magical capital of Elestra, where the great Elestra Academy of Magic, the State Library of Magia, the Magical Archives, and the Magical Reservoir would all be located.

The leaders created a huge fountain which drew water from the Magical Wells in each kingdom. The magical water that flows through the statues of the great heroes of each realm provides the magical power for Amemnop. The Six Kingdoms exist in harmony on Elestra. As long as they work together, a great power flows through our world and helps to keep Eldrack away."

"Where are we now?" Deanna asked.

"You're in the kitchen at Glabber's Grub Hut," Iszarre replied with a confused look.

"No," Deanna said, "I mean which Kingdom are we in?"

"Oh, yes, I see," Iszarre said. "You are in Magia. Amemnop is the largest city in Magia. The city is very powerful, but the darkness has disrupted Amemnop's harmony. When Eldrack stopped the fountain, he blocked most of our use of magic. I've spent years trying to figure out what spell he used, but nothing fits. There is no spell which would stop the fountain and block light from coming into the city."

"Where is the fountain?" Deanna asked.

"That I can show you," Iszarre said.

Suddenly, they heard a soft click as the door to the dining room closed. They knew that someone had been standing by the door listening to them.

Iszarre reached into a pot and pulled out a wooden spoon. He saw the children looking at him and he said, "I have to be ready for anything."

He pushed past them, motioning for them to be quiet, and opened the door. Derek followed and then Deanna came next. She clutched the wand tightly, but did not know any spells that would be useful if they were attacked.

As soon as they came out of the kitchen, they heard a man yell, "There they are. There are the Guardians."

Before they knew what was happening, two bolts of red flame shot at them from across the room. Iszarre held up his wooden spoon and caught the energy from the air. He swirled the spoon around and shot even larger bolts back at the two attackers. The two men were knocked against the wall. They dropped their wands but were able to stand up and run to the exit.

"You haven't won. Eldrack will hear about this," one of the men yelled.

"Let him come," Iszarre bellowed. "We will be ready." He saw that Derek, Deanna, and Tobungus had huddled behind the counter. "Come now, I will show you to the Fountain."

They got up a bit shakily and came around the counter. They saw that the snake Glabber was still devouring the butter, as if he had not noticed the magical battle that went on around him.

"Wait a second," Iszarre turned back to the kitchen. "I have to get the dishes that I was preparing out to the customers before we go."

They all followed him back into the kitchen and noticed that the old wizard looked even more angry than when they were attacked.

"What's wrong?" Deanna asked.

"When we left the kitchen, the peekaboo peppers escaped." He poked his wooden spoon at a few of the plates, but found nothing. "Oh, well, they're probably hidden in some of these dishes."

He used a levitation spell to pick up a tray with six plates of food and told the kids that he would be right back. When he returned, he loaded the rest of the finished plates on his tray and led everyone out into the dining room.

"Ahhh," a man yelled. Deanna and Derek turned to see the man's face turn a bright shade of red. They watched as a tiny maroon pepper snuck out from under his food, shouted "peekaboo," and scampered away into the kitchen.

"Why do you have those peppers in your kitchen?" Derek asked laughing.

"They're very popular in birthday cakes and in breakfast food," Iszarre explained. "When people are tired, they have to wake up and watch out for the peppers."

"How did you do that with a wooden spoon, when those guys attacked us?" Deanna asked.

"It's a wand shaped like a wooden spoon," Iszarre answered. "Since I cook so much, I thought I should have a spoon that can act as a wand."

"I thought I might have to use my lemon," Tobungus said seriously.

Derek was about to laugh, when Iszarre said thoughtfully, "Save the lemon for a real emergency, Tobungus." At Derek's look of surprise, he explained to the twins that a lemon could be a powerful magical weapon against a dark wizard like Eldrack.

Tobungus realized that Iszarre was right and put his lemon back in his minimizing bag. Immediately, he became lost in the bag, looking for something else buried with the rest of his stuff.

"Aren't you afraid that Eldrack will come here looking for you?" Derek asked.

"I have faced Eldrack before," Iszarre said mysteriously.

"Are you a Mystical Guardian too?" Deanna asked.

"No, I came before the Mystical Guardians. In fact, I chose the first Guardians." He saw that Deanna looked surprised. "I am 426 years old. I was the High Wizard of Magia three centuries ago. I fought Eldrack when he was young and made many mistakes. I realized that he would grow more powerful and that I needed help, so I selected a particularly powerful family to become the Mystical Guardians."

"That would be our family," Derek said.

"Yes, fifteen generations ago, one of your ancestors, Baladorn, defeated another great wizard in a tournament. He proved himself to be the mightiest of all wizards in Magia. He was given the title Baladorn the Mighty. Baladorn did much to defend Elestra from dark wizards, but after he faced Eldrack here in Amemnop, he disappeared. I have searched for Baladorn for almost three hundred years, but I have never found him."

"He's up in the cave above the city with our grandfather," Deanna said sadly. She told him the whole story of their arrival and their grandfather's warnings. "Can you rescue all of the Guardians?"

Iszarre shook his head. "I wish I could. The Cave of Imprisonment moves around Elestra. The only reason it was there when you arrived is that your grandfather was able to hold it in place so that you could come to Amemnop. By now, the cave will have moved to a new location."

"Then we really do have to find all of the moonstones before we can go home," Derek said softly.

"Yes," Iszarre said, "so let's get you to the Fountain of the Six Kingdoms."

6 Night Flight of the Birdmen

Iszarre led Deanna and Derek into the street and pointed to the north. "The fountain is on the other side of town, but I think we should stop by the library to learn more about the fountain. We need to figure out what Baladorn meant by the fountain remaining silent."

"I love libraries," Deanna said. She was thinking of the days that she and Derek had spent reading books on the cushy beanbag chairs at their town's library, where their aunt was the children's librarian.

"Well, you'll love this library," Iszarre said. "It has thousands of regular books, but it also has a large collection of magical books that can answer your questions, if you know what to ask. There are also lots of surprises in the library, if you take the time to look."

Derek was thinking that they should go straight to the fountain and try to figure out the mystery there. "Don't you think we should just head to the fountain?" he asked.

"No, we must go to the library," Iszarre said. "You will spend much time there, and you will learn more about Elestra from the books than you will from me. I think it's a good idea for you to get started there." He saw Derek's look of impatience and smiled at him, "Plus, Derek, you may enjoy exploring the darker places in the library on one of your visits."

"What do you mean?" Derek asked. "What kinds of dark places?"

"You and your sister are both Mystical Guardians, but it is likely that you will have slightly different powers," Iszarre said. "I suspect that one of your powers will be particularly useful in the library. But, I don't want to spoil any surprises, so let's get moving."

Derek hung back and thought about what Iszarre had said. He liked the idea of having some sort of mysterious magical power.

Iszarre walked quickly and the children were having trouble keeping up with him. "Wait," Tobungus called out. Derek thought that Tobungus was just too slow, but Tobungus pointed upward. Derek looked up and saw huge shadowy birds circling overhead.

"Iszarre," Derek cried, "what are those birds?"

Iszarre pulled his wooden spoon back out and said, "Get behind me kids. Those are Noctorns. They're kind of like flying coyote men, and they're not very nice. They can only come out in darkness because light hurts them."

Deanna looked up and saw that there were over one hundred of the frightening creatures swooping in to attack them. Iszarre pointed his spoon wand in the air and shouted, "Luminos vibratum."

A stream of yellow light shot up and hit one of the Noctorns. He shot another burst of magical light, but missed his next target. He tried to line up another Noctorn, but had to jump out of the way when one of the attackers threw a large rock down toward him.

"Come on," he called, heading further down the street. Derek, Deanna, and Tobungus followed him while trying to avoid the shower of stones that the Noctorns were raining down on them.

Iszarre ducked around a corner onto a narrow side street, and the kids followed. He peeked out and saw the Noctorns swoop up in a loop, regrouping before they continued their attack. Because the street they had turned on was narrower, the flying attackers had a harder time avoiding buildings and overhangs.

It didn't take long for the Noctorns to get more comfortable with the tighter spaces, however, and they started to rain stones down on the twins and their new friends once again. A small rock knocked Tobungus down, but he popped right back up and started running again. Another stone shattered a wooden sign. Deanna threw her hands in front of her face just in time to deflect the flying splinters.

Iszarre was frantically firing beams of light in the air behind him, but he missed with nearly every shot. As Derek watched Iszarre, he remembered that he was holding his flashlight and got a great idea. He pointed the flashlight upward and shined its light on one of the Noctorns.

The coyote-bird-man shrieked and fell to the ground with a thud. It slowly got up but was unable to start flying again. Derek called to the others and told them to get behind him. He swept the beam of his flashlight through the night sky and one Noctorn after another fell to the ground.

"What sort of magic is that?" Tobungus asked in awe.

"It's not magic. It's a flashlight," Derek yelled.

"I think I need to change my shoes," Tobungus said. He reached into his shoe bag and got a pair of running shoes. "Ha, now you'll see some speed. I'm the fastest fungus in Flestra," he bragged. Deanna just shook her head.

After a few minutes, Iszarre put his hand on Derek's shoulder and said, "We better get moving again." They looked to the area where Iszarre was pointing and saw that thirty or forty of the Noctorns had landed and were running toward them. Derek aimed his flashlight at them, but the beam would not work because he was not pointing it upward. Derek grabbed Deanna's hand and followed Iszarre and Tobungus down the street.

The Noctorns were slow, so they fell behind quickly. When the Noctorns were about a block behind, Iszarre turned and aimed his spoon down the street. He said, "*Edify escola.*" Sparks flew from his spoon wand and a shimmering wall formed across the street.

The first Noctorns reached the wall and bounced off of it. The rest stopped and seemed to be deciding what to do next. One of the Noctorns flapped his wings and jumped over the wall. He began walking toward Iszarre who sent another beam of yellow light which knocked the attacker to his knees.

Derek realized that the other Noctorns were about to jump over the wall in a group, so he ran back to the wall and laid on the ground with his flashlight shining upward. As the Noctorns appeared over the wall, he lit each one up and watched as they fell to the ground around him, too dazed to continue their attack. He was swinging his flashlight wildly around the top of the wall, when he heard Iszarre say, "It's over, Derek. The rest of the Noctorns are running away."

Derek stood up and rejoined the group. They walked through the streets of Amemnop for another twenty minutes before Iszarre told them that they had arrived. Derek and Deanna looked to their right and found that they were standing in front of the Library.

7 No Library Card Needed

Deanna and Derek followed Iszarre and Tobungus through the fifteen foot tall doors at the front of the State Library of Magia. Deanna nearly dropped the Wand of Ondarell when she saw the amazing sight that awaited them inside the dark building.

Hundreds of candles let out bits of light that danced across the walls of books that rose as high as she could see. The main room was at least five stories high and the bookshelves covered every inch of the walls, except for a series of small windows up near the ceiling.

Deanna tried to count the shelves, but lost track at sixty-four. Instead of starting over, she just stared, with her mouth hanging open. Derek waved his hand in front of her face and said, "Earth to Deanna. Hello in there."

She blinked her eyes and sighed, "Wow."

"Yes, Deanna, it's great that this library has thousands of books, but there's a flock of psycho coyote-bird-men somewhere in the city and a certain dark wizard named Eldrack may be on his way. I think we need to find out about the fountain as fast as possible."

She slowly came back to her senses and followed Derek to the desk where Iszarre seemed to be talking to himself. When they came up next to him, they saw that he was actually talking to a six inch woman with wings on her back who was standing on the desk. The tiny woman stood on a plaque that said, *Head Librarian.*

"I don't know which book I need," Iszarre said to the librarian. "There must be something that talks about how the fountain was built or who built it. We're trying to figure out why the fountain is silent."

"Hmm," the little woman muttered. "I suppose it's worth a try. Okay," she called out to no one in particular. "Show me books that discuss the construction of the Fountain of the Six Kingdoms."

A shower of sparks shot from a row of torches along the wall and dozens of books glowed on their shelves. "Book Fairies!" she called, "Retrieve the books!"

A swarm of tiny fairies exploded from under the desk and flew to the lighted books. The fairies were two inches tall and had clear wings that gave off a silvery glow. As the fairies flew, a trail of golden sparks followed them.

Within seconds, the books floated onto a stack on a nearby table. Iszarre thanked the Fairy Librarian for her help and offered chairs to the others. They all sat around the table, not knowing where to start. Finally, he touched his wand to the cover of one of the books and said "*Explanatum*." The book shook slightly and sat still.

"Okay," he said, "tell me about the silence of the Fountain of the Six Kingdoms."

The book's cover flew open and the pages whizzed by until the book stood open to page 127. A deep, raspy voice said,

> *The Prophecy of Baladorn says that Amemnop will remain dark as long as the Fountain remains quiet.*

"Yes, yes, we know that," Iszarre said impatiently. "But what does it mean?"

The book sounded embarrassed when it said, "I don't really know."

"Fat lot of good you are," Iszarre whispered. "Well, be off with you."

The book flew sadly back to its place on the shelves. He went from one book to another, but none contained the answers they so desperately needed. He grew angrier with each dead end and sat back to try to think of a new set of questions to ask the books.

Deanna wondered whether the Book of Spells in her charm could also talk, so she opened the charm and the book magically appeared. She touched the wand to the cover and whispered "*Explanatum.*" Nothing happened.

Iszarre reached over and touched her hand. "You have to believe in your power, Deanna. Remember, you are a Guardian, so the power is inside you."

She took a deep breath and touched the wand to the book again. "*Explanatum,*" she said loudly. The book shuddered, and she smiled widely. "Do you know a spell to break the Spell of Darkness which Eldrack has placed on Amemnop?"

The cover flew open and the book's ancient pages fluttered in a wind that did not exist. When they got to page 342, the book stopped moving and said:

The Spell of Darkness can be broken by a shower of magical water. The largest source of magical water in Amemnop is the Fountain of the Six Kingdoms. The Fountain sits above a powerful magical spring. Only an item of great magical power could stop the Fountain from flowing. You must first find the source of this magic. Then, once the Fountain begins to flow again, you must cast the Spell of Upward Rain to drive away the darkness.

The book went on to tell Deanna the magical words that she would need for her spell. She said the words *Precipitato magicum* under her breath over and over so that she would remember them when she got to the fountain.

Iszarre looked at Deanna and said, "That was very interesting. A magical item is blocking the Fountain. What do you suppose that meant?" he asked with a gleam in his eye.

"The moonstone," Deanna blurted out. "It has to be the moonstone. Somehow, Baladorn hid it in the Fountain." She had a confused look on her face. "But why would he hide it there?"

"He probably knew that he would be captured and did not want Eldrack to get the moonstone too. He hid it near the Fountain because he knew that anyone trying to break the Spell of Darkness would need the power within the moonstone to make their own spell work." Iszarre sat back and sighed deeply, "But we still don't know what Baladorn meant by the Fountain remaining silent."

"I have an idea," Derek said excitedly. He asked Deanna for the wand and once he had it, he touched the tip to the nearest book and said, "*Explanatum.*" The book shuddered and he said, "Tell me if you know anything about the Fountain of the Six Kingdoms making noise when it shoots water. Does it make any sort of whistling sound?"

The book flew open to page 119. A high woman's voice said:

> *People who have seen the Fountain when it was still flowing say that it makes a haunting music, like a strong wind blowing through a forest.*

"I knew it! Thank you," Derek said to the book.

The book replied, "You are quite a gentleman, unlike the rude man over there."

A leather strip in the book fluttered like a tongue toward Iszarre who looked embarrassed. He knew that he had been unkind to the books, and he decided that he would come back later and explain the situation. Perhaps he would bring a gift, not butter, but something like a nice bookmark.

"What did we just figure out?" Deanna asked.

Derek handed the wand back to her and said, "The Fountain's music is really just air rushing through the pipes above the spring. The air probably is like a vacuum that pulls the water through the Fountain."

He was growing more confident that his idea was correct. He continued, "I was helping Uncle Mike with that turtle fountain he has in his backyard, and I remember it making a wheezing sound because the air was blocking the water. The question is, what has happened to the water that should still be coming up through the spring?"

"Yeah, I remember that," Deanna said. "It sounded like the turtle was trying to cough up a hairball.

"I suppose we should get going to the Fountain to figure out what has happened to the water from the spring," Iszarre said as he pushed himself up from his seat. "You may want to tell your friend to get ready."

Derek looked over and saw that Tobungus had set at least ten pairs of shoes out on the next table and was trying to decide which pair to wear. Finally, he said, "I still need speed, but we could get wet by the Fountain. I think these hiking boots will do nicely." He put his shoes on and followed Iszarre, Derek, and Deanna back into the street.

Iszarre breathed deeply and sighed, "It's turning into a beautiful night. I know you can't see it through the darkness, but the first moon will be directly overhead soon."

Before Derek or Deanna could reply, a booming voice called, "Iszarre, we meet again." They looked down the street and saw a tall man in a flowing black cape with glowing orange eyes.

Behind them, Iszarre whispered, "Eldrack."

8 An Obstacle Course and an Obstinate Horse

"Come on, kids!" Iszarre yelled, running down the street away from Eldrack. They raced after him with Tobungus on their heels.

"It's a good thing I chose the hiking boots," their mushroom friend yelled. "Hey, Iszarre!" he called, "what time is it?"

"What?" Iszarre replied. "What do you mean?"

"It's lemon time!" Tobungus squealed, reaching back over his shoulder into his smaller bag.

"No, Tobungus," Iszarre yelled, "save the lemon until you can be sure to hit Eldrack."

"Alright," Tobungus said disappointedly. He looked back and saw that Eldrack was gaining on them. Deanna had found an alley which cut over one street and put them closer to the fountain. As Tobungus entered the alley, a blast from Eldrack's wand splintered the wooden sidewalk behind him. "Iszarre!" he cried.

Iszarre looked back and saw Eldrack sending spell after spell at Tobungus and the children. He yelled for them to run through a park that was thick with bushes and trees. They wound through the bushes, preventing Eldrack from getting a clean shot at them.

Derek looked over at Iszarre and saw him desperately trying to block Eldrack's lightning bolt spells. "I thought you defeated Eldrack the last time you faced him!" Derek yelled, as they slipped behind a stand of bushes.

"That was a very long time ago," Iszarre replied. "Eldrack has grown more powerful and there is very little magic flowing through Amemnop these days."

"Where's Tobungus?" Deanna called out. They peered out from the bushes they were using as hiding places and saw no sign of the mushroom man. Instead, they saw Eldrack step out from behind a nearby tree and raise his wand to send a final spell at them.

Just then, they heard the whinnies of horses and saw Tobungus sitting atop a beautiful white horse. The horse jumped through the bushes behind Eldrack and knocked him to the ground. A second horse followed him.

"You have horses in Elestra?" Derek asked in surprise.

"You will find that our worlds share many things." Iszarre replied mysteriously.

Tobungus brought the horse alongside Iszarre and said, "Hop on!" Derek and Deanna climbed onto the second horse and rode after Tobungus. They heard him tell Iszarre that there was a third horse just around the bend and that he was afraid Eldrack might use it to catch them.

As they passed the third horse, Iszarre held his spoon wand out and said, "*Slumbero*." The horse dropped his head and leaned against the fence next to it. "That should hold him for a while."

Deanna looked back and saw Eldrack climbing onto the horse. "Ya!" he called, but the horse stumbled sideways and let out a short "bluh" sound. Eldrack kicked the animal to get him moving, but the horse could only stumble forward slowly.

Eldrack dismounted and looked at the horse to try to figure out what Iszarre had done to it. The horse raised his head and said "bluh" again. Eldrack saw the young Guardians disappearing on the other horses and angrily yelled, "Nocto!"

A small flock of Noctorns swooped past him toward the escaping horses.

"Derek! The Noctorns are back!" Deanna called above the whipping wind. Derek whistled to get Tobungus' attention. He turned down a narrow alley, and the Noctorns had to rise up over the buildings.

As they emerged from the alley, they had to avoid a shower of stones being thrown at them from the flying menaces. Derek waved his flashlight upward and knocked several of the attackers down. They guided their horses through parks and under overhangs to evade the Noctorns which kept coming after them. Up ahead, Derek saw a large building that looked like a mix between a barn and a small factory. The sign said that it was a blacksmith's shop.

Derek guided their horse toward the blacksmith's shop and grabbed a red-hot iron as they passed. He tossed it into a barrel of cold water and heard the hiss of steam rise. Iszarre saw what he was doing and used a spell to pick up all of the molten metal pieces and drop them into the water. Billowing clouds of hot steam rose and forced the Noctorns to slow down and change directions.

They raced on toward the Fountain, and when they were close, Tobungus said, "You guys jump off and I'll take the horses around the block. The Noctorns should follow me."

Derek, Deanna, and Iszarre hopped off of the horses and waited under a nearby building's overhang. The sounds of the Noctorns' heavy wings beating the air faded. After a few seconds, Iszarre looked out and said that it was all clear. They walked quickly toward the fountain, which they saw was only a block away.

Derek and Deanna were hoping that they would reach the Fountain without any more problems, when suddenly they heard Eldrack's booming voice. "There they are! The girl has the wand!"

Iszarre waved them over to a stone wall just in front of the Fountain. They peeked out and saw Eldrack, the two men who had attacked them at the diner, and a growing flock of Noctorns moving down the street toward them.

"We need help," Iszarre said solemnly.

"Listen," Deanna said. They tilted their heads and heard the clopping feet of a horse in the distance. Moments later, they saw the white stallion with Tobungus, but he was not alone. A huge snake was coiled behind him.

"Glabber," Iszarre whispered. "Well, we've got our help."

"What good will a snake do against Eldrack?" Derek asked.

"Glabber is a powerful wizard who originally came from the Desert Realm. We have worked together for years to watch over Amemnop. Eldrack knows that he must use hot spells against me, but cold spells against Glabber. He'll have to divide his spells between us."

"What do you mean by hot and cold spells?" Deanna asked.

"If Eldrack battles a human wizard, he must use lightning or fire spells like you saw earlier. Those are the hot spells. Reptile wizards absorb hot spells and get stronger from them, so Eldrack would have to use ice or snow spells. Those spells do little damage to me, so Eldrack will not be able to attack us both effectively."

Tobungus stopped the horse next to them, and he jumped off with Glabber. They all huddled behind the short wall and waited for Eldrack's first attack.

"Thanks for coming, Glabber," Deanna said.

"Well, I owed Tobungus. After all, he gave me a whole stick of butter." He swished his forked tongue across his cheeks and murmured, "A whole stick."

Derek chuckled to himself. Even though they were in danger from Eldrack, he was really beginning to like Elestra.

Iszarre looked at the children and said, "Deanna. Derek. Whatever you're going to do, you'd better get going." Derek looked behind them and saw the Fountain of the Six Kingdoms. The Fountain was made up of statues of great wizards, some human, some reptilian, and others with features they could not recognize.

Derek grabbed Deanna's hand and said, "Let's find that moonstone."

9 The Fountain and Youth

Deanna looked at the fountain and felt very small next to the huge statues of Elestra's great wizards. "I don't know where to start looking," she said to Derek.

"The spring is probably under the middle of the fountain," Derek replied. "We're going to have to wade into the water." Derek led the way into the middle of the fountain and shivered as the cold water soaked his pants. He reached the largest statue and began searching around its base. The darkness seemed magnified by the blackness of the water surrounding them.

Deanna could see his frustration and held the wand toward the statue and said *"Luminos vibratum."* Nothing happened. She had forgotten that light could not travel downward with the shield of darkness still in place.

"Put the wand in the water before you use the spell," Iszarre yelled to her.

Deanna dunked her hand with the wand into the icy water and repeated, "*Luminos vibralum.*" Soft yellow light shot from the wand and allowed Derek to see into the water. He looked up at her in surprise and she said, "It's the same spell Iszarre used against the Noctorns."

As Derek started to search for the pipes that led into the fountain, they heard a chorus of zips and shrieks from magic spells being hurled between Eldrack and Iszarre and Glabber.

Deanna looked back and saw Eldrack sending spells wildly at Iszarre and Glabber. He must have been trying to get a lucky shot to hit one of them, so that he could then focus on the other wizard with only one type of magic. She wanted to help out, but she knew that she had to hold the wand steady to help Derek.

"I think I see it," Derek whispered. "The pipes wind around under this big guy's foot, but I see something orange blocking the pipe just above the water line." He reached down and pulled with all of his strength. "Urrgh," he grunted. "This. . . thing. . . won't. . . budge," he said, but he kept trying.

With Eldrack's wild attacks flying overhead, Derek pulled and yanked, and yanked and pulled, and finally, he felt the moonstone give way. With one final tug, he pulled it out. He heard a whoosh of air flow through the fountain's pipes.

"No!" Eldrack yelled. "Nocto! Nocto! Nocto!" He turned to Iszarre and hissed, "They'll never get the fountain working."

A swarm of Noctorns appeared overhead and began diving toward the fountain. "Deanna," Derek called. He tossed the moonstone to her and said, "Now, it's your turn." He grabbed his flashlight and aimed at the incoming birdmen.

Iszarre looked over and saw the wave of Noctorns descending toward Deanna and turned to Tobungus. "Now, my friend. It's lemon time."

"Woohoo!" Tobungus shouted. He reached into his bag and grabbed the lemon. He hopped into the fountain and ran to Derek's side.

"What are you going to do with that?" Derek asked.

"Watch and learn, Dripsy," he answered. He split the lemon open and squeezed its juice on the statues surrounding them. After one last squeeze, he yelled, "*Citros.*"

A shimmering shield pulsated above them and knocked the first Noctorns twenty feet beyond the fountain's edges. "You better hurry," he said, "the lemon juice is pretty watered down from the fountain. This shield will only last another five minutes or so."

Deanna saw that water was dribbling out of the fountain, but the fountain was not coming back on at full strength. She remembered that the book said that the magical water had to hit the shield of darkness. "Tobungus, did you say you have a cup in that bag of yours?" she asked.

Tobungus swung his bag off of his shoulder and pulled out a small metal cup. He handed it to her and wondered what she had in mind.

Deanna filled the cup with the water that lapped at their legs and tossed it upward. Nothing happened. She thought furiously. Why had the water not worked? "A *shower* of magical water," she whispered. "The water has to hit the shield of darkness from above."

She turned to Iszarre and yelled, "I need to know a spell to freeze water and another to melt ice."

"*Hydro Fridgin* will do the freezing and *Infernum* will melt it," he called back.

She filled the cup again and pointed the wand at the water. *"Hydro Fridgin,"* she said in a strong voice. The water swirled in the cup and began to freeze. She held the cup up and Derek put his hands underneath it. She dumped a perfect snowball out and said, "Aim above the middle of the fountain and throw it as high as you can."

Derek took a deep breath and wound up like a baseball pitcher. He threw the snowball as high as he could and when it reached its highest point, Deanna pointed the wand at it and shouted, *"Infernum!"*

The snowball exploded into a thousand drops of water that rained down on the shield of darkness. The area of the shield that had been hit shimmered and disappeared. Starlight and one of Elestra's moons peeked through the small hole in the city's black ceiling.

Deanna was relieved that the spells had worked, but Tobungus shouted, "The lemon shield is weakening! The Noctorns will be able to get through any second."

"Derek, cover me with the flashlight," she called.

Derek aimed his flashlight upward and picked off a few Noctorns that tried to attack Deanna.

She climbed up the wizard statue directly under the hole in the shield and reached into her pocket for the moonstone. She expected Eldrack to turn his attacks toward her, but he never raised his wand in her direction.

"No!" Eldrack yelled again, only in a more desperate tone.

Deanna remembered what Iszarre had said about gaining power by looking through the moonstone. She looked at the dark wizard and then held the moonstone in front of her eyes. She turned her head to look at the moon and as soon as it was in view, a blanket of orange light wrapped around her. A few seconds later, the light was gone and she put the moonstone into her pocket.

She stood up confidently and aimed the wand down toward the pool of magical water. "*Precipitato Magicum,*" she said, repeating the spell she had memorized at the library. A wave of sound and light shot down into the water. The water rose like a curtain and rained down on the rest of the shield above the fountain.

Now uncovered, the fountain sprang back to life. The wizard statues shot water in all directions carving small rivers along the streets leading away from the fountain.

"You haven't won yet," Eldrack yelled. "There's not enough magic in Amemnop to drop the rest of the shield."

Deanna saw that the water was flowing throughout the city and called back, "The magic is in the water." She aimed the wand down again and yelled, "*Precipitato Magicum*."

All over Amemnop, curtains of water rose up and fell back down like rain on the shield of darkness. The shield withered and disappeared, leaving the whole city open to the night sky for the first time in three hundred years.

As light began to shine in the city again, the residents came out of their homes and stores. They headed to the fountain and saw Eldrack backing away toward the edge of town.

"We will meet again," the dark wizard cried, "and I will have that wand." One of the Noctorns swooped down and picked him up. He rode high into the sky and disappeared with the rest of the flying beasts.

Deanna handed the moonstone to Derek and said, "You better look through it too." He held the moonstone up to his eyes and felt a wave of magic flow through him.

One of the city's residents called out that they should follow Eldruck, but Iszarre held up his hand and said that they should focus on returning Amemnop to its glory.

After talking with Glabber for a moment, Iszarre turned to Derek, Deanna, and Tobungus, and said, "Let's go back to the diner to talk and get something to eat."

They were soaked and cold, but they were excited that they had beaten their new enemy in their first battle. Everything about Amemnop seemed to be changing around them. They could feel the magic floating on the breeze, and their confidence swelled. It wasn't a dark city that looked abandoned.

As they walked through the city to Glabber's Grub Hut, they saw people taking the boards off of their windows. The city was now bright from the lights streaming from houses and stores. Amemnop seemed to be coming back to life.

10 City of Light

Derek and Deanna settled into chairs at a table near the counter at Glabber's Grub Hut. With the excitement in the streets, the diner was empty. Tobungus stood next to the table checking to see if any of his shoes had fallen out of his bag. Deanna noticed that he looked sad and thought that it might have something to do with a missing shoe.

Iszarre and Glabber brought out a tray of food that covered the entire table. Derek reached for a plate of pizza and Deanna grabbed a milkshake. "I'm a little surprised that you have the same type of food here in Elestra that we have back home," Derek said between bites.

"We don't usually," Iszarre said. "I've been to your world many times, so I know what your people like to eat."

"Why have you been to our world?" Deanna asked.

"I am a member of the High Council that oversees all magical activities in Barado's Kingdom. That requires me to go to your world from time to time." He paused for a second. "That's how I know your father."

Derek dropped his pizza. "You know our dad?"

"Oh yes, I know him. I have warned him that he must stay away from Elestra because he would be the fourteenth generation of Guardians. I'm afraid that he may come here now, since he will soon find out that you are both here. I've sent a message to him, letting him know that you are safe and that you have found the first moonstone. Hopefully, that will reassure him."

"If he comes here, he'll be in danger," Derek said.

"Yes, and he knows that. You must keep going and find the rest of the moonstones. If you collect them all, you will be able to wake the other Guardians and defeat Eldrack. That is the best way to protect your father. Your father has gone through his magical training, so Eldrack would be able to sense his arrival in Elestra. You two have not started yet, so he will have trouble finding you."

"I think we'll stick out like a sore thumb," Derek said.

"Oh, I don't think so," Iszarre replied. "There are so many strange things here in Elestra to distract people. You'll blend in easily." He sat back and stroked his beard, deep in thought. "I was also able to get a message to your mother," he added.

"I was wondering about that," Deanna said. "Is our mother a Guardian also?"

"No," Iszarre said slowly, "but she does come from a powerful family here in Elestra. It is no surprise that you two are twins. Your mother has 46 sisters, and one brother."

"What!?!" exclaimed Deanna and Derek in surprise.

Iszarre continued as if they had not interrupted him. "All of the sisters come from sets of twins, but they are different from twins in your world. In her family, only one twin ages at a time. In fact, with most of them, one of the twins gets older very quickly, while the other stays young for a long time. It's impossible to know how old any of them are because two sisters can be twins and still be 300 years apart in age. Plus, they can go to the Antikrom Mountains and age in reverse, so it's really hard to tell their age."

"That doesn't make any sense," Derek said.

"Exactly," said Iszarre. "Elestra is full of weird things, and you'll just have to learn to accept that."

"But, we've never heard about her sisters, except for our aunt who comes to visit around the holidays," Derek said.

"That's not surprising," Iszarre said, "most of them stay here in Elestra, and it would be pretty strange if you heard that your mother had 46 sisters."

"And one brother," Deanna reminded him.

"Yes, and one brother," Iszarre murmured. He saw the kids eyeing him, and added, "Her brother has not joined the sisters in their work. He has chosen to be a yak herder. He spends his days on a farm high in the Antikrom Mountains, away from the battle with Eldrack."

"What work do our mother's sisters do?" Deanna asked.

"That is something that I cannot tell you," Iszarre said. "They will let you know about their mission a bit at a time. You will surely run into them here in Elestra, and when you do, you may be able to figure out about their Sisterhood."

Derek and Deanna sat back, thinking about what they had learned.

"There is one thing you might be able to tell me," Deanna said before Iszarre could get up to leave. "Why are some spells from the Book of Spells so long, while others are just one or two words?"

"You see, Deanna," Iszarre began, "your Book of Spells is for your wand, and only your wand. The wand knows some spells, so the Book can include only the shorter form of the spell."

"The wand knows the spells?" Deanna asked.

"Well, not exactly," Iszarre corrected. "Over time, a wizard forms a bond with the wand. When the wizard uses a spell many times, the wand remembers it, and the wizard can make the spell happen more quickly. The longer spells in the Book are the spells that the wand has not been told to perform in the past."

"I get it," Derek said. "So, if Deanna uses a spell a bunch of times, she can use a shortcut to make the spell work again."

"Exactly!" Iszarre said. "There are even stories of the most powerful wizards from deep in the past being able to simply tell their wands what to do without using magical words, but I have never seen that happen."

Deanna nodded that she understood what Iszarre had told her, but she was getting nervous about their next adventure.

Iszarre sensed her mood and said, "You two will learn how to work with the wand as you search from the moonstones."

"But we don't know what to do next," Deanna blurted out, showing her frustration. "We have no idea where any of the moonstones are hidden."

"First, you will sleep. Then, tomorrow morning, you can explore Amemnop. When the sun sets and the first moons rise, I will take you to the Tower of the Moons where you will return the first moonstone to its place in the arch."

He settled into his chair more comfortably. "You see, there is a metal arch in the tower with slots for all fifteen moonstones. When they are all in place and the moons are lined up, you can concentrate the power of all of the moons at once. You have already looked through the moonstone and gained some power. When you return it to the arch, you can look through it again, and you will see a vision of the final moments when the stone's Guardian had it. This might give you some clues about what sorts of magic Eldrack likes to use and what works against him."

"But, we didn't see any visions when we looked through the moonstone in the fountain," Deanna said.

"It has to be in the arch," Iszarre replied. "After you return the first moonstone, you will have to return to the Library to discover where your next adventure will take you."

"Won't Eldrack learn that the moonstone is in the Tower and try to steal it?" Deanna asked, thinking that the moonstones should be held in a magical safe guarded by Iszarre and Glabber.

"He won't be able to," Iszarre answered. "The Tower is protected by magic that Eldrack does not understand. Once the moonstone is in place, he won't be able to get it out."

"Iszarre," Deanna said, "we heard our dad say something about our grandfather's moonstone being free when the sun rose. What did he mean?"

"When I chose your family to be Mystical Guardians, all fifteen moonstones were put in the arch with a spell that protected them while they were there. Each stone was for a different generation of Guardians, and each Guardian had a special day when the magic that protected the stone would wear off. They all knew that they had to get their stones on that day or Eldrack could take the stones without using magic."

"So, if our grandfather was captured when he came to Elestra, did Eldrack get his stone?" Deanna asked.

"No," Iszarre answered. "Your grandfather was able to see into the future, through a prophecy. He sent a second copy of himself to move the stone to its hiding place."

"How do you send a copy of yourself to do something?" Derek asked.

"It's very complicated. It takes many years of practice to learn how to use duplicating magic. When he entered the portal in your yard, he allowed the copy to break off and go to the moonstone."

"So, can we get the copy to help us?" Deanna asked.

"No," Iszarre replied. "The copy evaporated as soon as its job was done."

"Iszarre," Deanna said thoughtfully, "if the moonstones are taken out by the Guardian when the spell wears off, then how are they protected when they go back into the arch?"

"Ah, Deanna," Iszarre said. "You are very clever. After reading a secret prophecy, I created a spell that would protect the moonstones if they were put back into the arch. I'm afraid that I can't tell you anything more specific."

Iszarre stroked his beard and continued, "You will find that many things in Elestra are foretold in prophecies. Sometimes, these prophecies describe unimportant events, but at other times, they tell us about key points in our history. We can learn about Eldrack's moves if we are very careful to read what the prophecies are trying to tell us. You will learn about prophecies during your time here, and you will understand why I must not say anything else."

Derek looked over and watched Tobungus sitting with his hands over his face. "He sure looks sad about something."

"I'll be right back," Iszarre said. He stood up and walked over to Tobungus.

Tobungus did not even look up or say anything. "It's alright," Iszarre began, "I know how much it meant to you."

"I've had that lemon for a long time," Tobungus said as tears started to flow down his cheeks. "I know I had to use it, but I feel so powerless without it."

"Well, if you're going to join Derek and Deanna on their next journey, I certainly don't want you to be powerless."

He reached into his flowing robes and pulled out a new lemon with his right hand and set it on the table in front of Tobungus who looked up in surprise. Iszarre pulled his left hand out and set a lime next to the lemon.

"I don't know what to say," Tobungus blurted out.

Iszarre smiled warmly and patted Tobungus on the hand. "Now, I won't be with you all the time, so you will have to protect the children, Tobungus."

"Absolutely," the giddy mushroom man squealed. He reached into his shoe bag and pulled out his tap shoes. As he tap danced around the diner, Iszarre went back to talk with Derek and Deanna.

Iszarre looked at Deanna and said, "You showed a great deal of power in the Fountain tonight. I had no idea that you would be able to use the Spell of Upward Rain so well." He turned to Derek and said, "You have proven your cleverness here in Amemnop. That will serve you well, but you must remember that you also have the magical power of the Mystical Guardians. Don't be afraid to use it."

"I won't," Derek said in a shaky voice.

Derek was ready to head up to bed, but Deanna had a worried look on her face. "What's the matter?" Iszarre asked.

"Why didn't Eldrack fire any spells at me when I was on the Fountain?" she asked softly.

"I don't know," replied Iszarre. "Maybe he was only paying attention to Glabber and me."

Deanna shook her head slowly. Eldrack had looked at her. He had spoken to her, but he made no move to attack her. For some reason that bothered her, but she did not know why.

Iszarre showed the children to their room on the second floor of the diner's building. The room looked exactly like their room at home.

Iszarre smiled. "I wanted you to feel comfortable here, so I made a copy of your room. Simple magic really. I made sure that there are plenty of clothes in the dressers. If you want to change the colors of your clothes, you will find a convenient spell for that in the charm." He winked at Deanna.

They thanked Iszarre and got ready for bed. They fell asleep quickly and dreamed of dragons flying in the skies above their yard back home.

The First Vision

Derek and Deanna woke up late the next morning. When they came downstairs, Iszarre had breakfast waiting for them. They hungrily gulped bites of strawberry flavored French toast and drank a thick green juice that tasted much better than it looked.

Derek stopped suddenly and started coughing. Deanna saw his face turning red.

"What's the matter, Derek?" she asked.

Before he could answer, she heard a squeaky voice shout, "Peek-a-boo!" A tiny pepper struggled out from the French toast and rolled off of the table before running back into the kitchen.

"Iszarre!" Deanna yelled toward the kitchen.

The old wizard rushed out with his spoon wand ready to face more of Eldrack's minions, but he saw that she had called about Derek biting into a peek-a-boo pepper. He chuckled and said, "*Infernius expellus.*"

An icy blast crossed Derek's tongue, and the fiery heat of the pepper was gone. Iszarre saw that Derek looked angry. "Hey," he said, "I thought you would need help waking up after your adventure yesterday."

"Thanks, but I can wake myself up," Derek replied. Derek drank almost a whole glass of the green juice to get the remaining pepper flavor off of his tongue. He poked his French toast and asked if there were any more peppers hidden in them.

"No, there was only the one pepper," Iszarre said. "One is usually enough to do the job." He patted Derek on the shoulder and sat down at the table with them. "I think it's time to tell you two more about Elestra so that you will be ready for anything."

He cleared his throat to keep from laughing and continued, "Deep underground, at the very core of Elestra, is a huge ruby. This is not just any ruby though. It is pure magic. The magic from the Ruby Core flows upward to the surface of Elestra. Every once in a while, a tiny fragment of the solid ruby breaks off and shoots out of a well. These rubies are often used in magical staffs, amulets, and wands, because they have such concentrated magic."

Iszarre took a sip of tea that was bubbling and spitting wisps of steam into the air. He continued, "Each of the Six Kingdoms has a protected well which lets the magic flow upward. I'm afraid that when Eldrack becomes powerful enough, he will try to block the wells and remove all magic from Elestra. If he does that, he will be able to defeat King Barado easily."

"What about the magic from the Fountain?" Deanna asked.

"That magic seems powerful, but it is very small next to the magic that flows from the wells."

"What does Eldrack's battle with King Barado have to do with our world?" Derek asked.

"The magic from the Six Kingdoms produces clouds that swirl through the skies of Elestra. The moons travel through the clouds. The cloud that covers a moon determines what each world is like."

"Wait a minute," Derek interrupted. "We don't live on a moon. We live on Earth. It's a planet that has its own moon."

"Of course," Iszarre said. "The moons are not really moons like you're used to. They're more like their own realm where many worlds exist together. People live on all of Elestra's moons, but your world and many others lie beyond the moons."

"So, are the moons and the worlds that exist by them like a solar system?" Deanna asked.

"No," Iszarre explained. "The moons that you see in Elestra's sky act as gateways. Your world and many others lie beyond those gateways. Each moon is a gateway to many worlds. Elestra is the magical center of all of these worlds."

"I think I understand," Derek said, but he knew that he really didn't fully understand what Iszarre was explaining.

Iszarre put his hand on Derek's shoulder and said, "You will learn more about the moons and come to understand their connection to the outworlds as you travel through Elestra. But for now, I will just give you a bit more information. Your world has gone through ice ages when the cloud from the Icelands covered your world. Then, you went through a period with dragons and wizards, when the clouds from the Sky Dragons and Magia dominated. Now, clouds from the Desert Realm, Oceania, and the Forest Kingdom are about evenly spread over your world. If Eldrack defeats Barado, he will be able to alter your world."

"Do you know where the rest of the moonstones are?" Derek asked. He wondered whether Iszarre had any ideas about the locations of the other moonstones.

"I hear things," Iszarre replied. "I can tell you that you will travel to each of the Six Kingdoms and will experience new types of magic that you have never imagined before. There is so much for you to learn, and so much that I simply can't tell you yet. But, I can tell you this, you will be in a race against Eldrack to find the moonstones, and I am sure that you will always be there for each other and combine your skills to defeat him."

After breakfast, Iszarre took the twins on a tour of Amemnop. They saw the Magian Magical Research Academy, where wizards were constantly trying new spells and potions, the Elestran Hoverball Hall of Fame, the Magian Zoo and Bestiary, and a street fair that popped up to celebrate the return of light to Amemnop.

As they walked along Amemnop's streets, they noticed that the buildings seemed to be changing colors. The dull gray walls were becoming brightly colored. The streets and sidewalks seemed less dusty, and there were people moving about.

Iszarre stopped by a street vendor and bought dinner dice and drinks for himself and the twins. Deanna was about to take a bite of one of the soft dice, when Iszarre stopped her. "You have to roll the dice first," he said.

She looked unsure, but gently rolled the dice. A four appeared, and she picked it up and took a bite. "Mmm, this tastes like pizza," she said. "I'm not sure what the toppings are, but this is good."

Derek quickly rolled one of his dice and got a two. He took a bite, expecting the same pizza, but instead, he tasted something that reminded him of spicy chili. "What is it about me and spicy food today?" he asked. He carefully took another bite and realized that the chili was not too spicy, so he ate the rest of the small cube.

"You never know what you're going to get until you roll the dice," Iszarre explained. "And, if you roll two at the same time, you get even more possibilities." They all sat rolling their dice, being surprised by what they tasted, as the light in the sky faded.

When dusk had fully gripped Amemnop, Iszarre took the twins to the Tower of the Moons which rose higher than any other building in Amemnop. Before opening the door, he sighed and lowered his head. Derek and Deanna were not sure what he was thinking, but he looked worried and relieved at the same time. He quickly took a deep breath, smiled reassuringly at them, and pushed the door open.

They entered the Tower of the Moons and walked to the top on a spiral staircase that wound around the inside of the tower's walls. The rest of the inside of the tower was empty, except that in the very center of the tower, another spiral staircase wound tightly up to the top.

It took twenty minutes to reach the top, and when they did, Iszarre had to rest for a few minutes. He finally waved them into a room that was just under the Tower's spire-like roof. They saw a thick bronze strip of metal arching overhead from one side of the room to the other. Fifteen slots were spaced along the arch in sets of three. Iszarre pointed to the slot nearest the north wall.

Deanna walked over and dug the moonstone out of her pocket. She snapped it in place on the arch and stepped back to look at how much of their journey still lay ahead of them.

"Go ahead," Iszarre said. "Look through the moonstone."

The twins looked at the shimmering moonstone and saw a wavy image of the spiral staircases in the tower. On the staircase that hugged the outer walls of the tower, two figures raced toward the top. One of them looked like Baladorn, and the other was a tall man they had never seen.

On the middle staircase, Eldrack ran to the top. He was firing spells at Baladorn, who was able to trip Eldrack with a lucky shot.

Baladorn got a lead and reached the top first. He plucked the orange moonstone from the arch that held all fifteen stones and held it high in the air. Suddenly, Eldrack popped through a trapdoor in the floor and fired a spell at Baladorn's hand. The moonstone flew out of the tower and into the night, and its orange light disappeared in the darkness.

A huge black bird swooped in and grabbed it out of the air and began to fly off. Baladorn watched in fear as his moonstone disappeared. Without warning, a blast of light like lightning shot from somewhere on the ground in Amemnop and hit the bird. The moonstone fell into the darkness. Eldrack watched what had happened and screamed in anger. He turned to attack Baladorn but found that he and the other man had disappeared.

"You just saw the moment when Baladorn took his moonstone from the arch," Iszarre said.

"Who was that man with Baladorn?" Derek asked.

"That was King Barado," Iszarre answered.

"Did the moonstone fall into the fountain?" Deanna asked.

"I don't know," Iszarre said. "When you have found more moonstones, your power will grow, and you will be able to see more details in the visions. As you can see from the spaces in the arch, the moonstones are placed in groups of three stones. Each time you complete a set of three stones, you can come back to a moonstone and see more details of the visions."

Iszarre looked away from the arch, as if he heard a faraway sound. "The grouping of the stones is connected to the five magical instruments of Elestra. Each set of stones comes together to give off the sounds of one instrument. When all of the stones are together and all of the magical instruments play together, the song will allow you to call a magical army that will help you in your final battle with Eldrack."

"Iszarre," Derek said, "I'm confused."

"About what?" Iszarre asked.

"When Baladorn went to get the moonstone from the arch, all fifteen stones were there," Derek said. "You told us that moonstones could only be taken out on a certain day by the wizard who was assigned to that stone." Iszarre nodded. "So, where are the final two moonstones? Shouldn't our dad's stone and our stone still be here?"

"Okay, I probably shouldn't tell you this until you have found a few more moonstones, but you are very clever," Iszarre said. "There is a second arch."

He saw the confused looks on the twins' faces. "I knew that it would be dangerous if Eldrack figured out how to get the moonstones. Once the Mystical Guardians started to disappear, I realized that I would have to separate the stones. Eldrack hasn't come to the Tower since his battle with Baladorn, so he doesn't know that the other stones were moved."

He put his hand on Deanna's shoulder and said, "And, he can't come back now that the magical protection has been renewed. After you have found the first fourteen stones, you will have to find the second arch to find your stone."

They walked back down the spiral staircase and into the bustling street. Iszarre led them back to Glabber's Grub Hut and stopped to speak with them before they went up to their room.

Deanna spoke first. "Will you come with us on our next adventure?"

"I don't know," he said. "You have turned Amemnop into the City of Light again. There is much magic here and I am growing more powerful with each passing hour. I will have to visit King Barado to tell him what has happened. I will watch your progress, and I will be there when you need me."

"What are we supposed to do alone?" Derek asked.

"You won't be alone. Tobungus will join you and you will make new friends. You will have a room and food at Glabber's place whenever you need it, and I will give you a bag of gold coins to take with you." He straightened up and said, "You are Mystical Guardians. You will never be alone in Elestra."

"I guess we should get some sleep. We have to get going early in the morning to the Library," Deanna said. "We have no idea what we're trying to find in those stubborn books."

"We will see each other again soon," Iszarre said. As they were about to climb the stairs, he called out, "You have a lot to learn about Elestra at the Library. When you're ready to search for the second moonstone, I think you should start by looking up the Baroka Valley." Deanna looked back and saw him smile with a twinkle in his eye.

Turn the page. The adventure continues…

Epilogue

Derek and Deanna found the first moonstone and defeated Eldrack in their first battle, but there is much more to do and much more to learn.

In their bits of free time, Deanna and Derek wandered through the State Library of Magia to find out more about the places, people, and creatures they encountered. The first three people they researched were Iszarre, Glabber, and Eldrack. The following pages will tell you what they learned, and perhaps, just as importantly, what they didn't learn.

Iszarre

Derek and Deanna spent the next day in the State Library of Magia researching the wizards they had met on their first day in Elestra. They asked the fairy librarian for books that would describe Iszarre.

The tiny fairy librarian ordered the book fairies to bring two books that would tell them everything they wanted to know. Before Deanna turned to sit down with Derek, the librarian said, "If you have a whole stack of books, you can use the *Explanatum* spell on the whole stack, and then you can just ask each book your questions."

"Thanks," Deanna said. "That makes things a bit easier."

"You're welcome," the librarian said. "There's no reason to have your wand out when you don't need it."

Deanna walked over to the table where Derek had set their bags and told him what the fairy librarian had told her. She turned to the two books on the table, waved her wand and said, "*Explanatum.*"

The first book was the *Elestran Encyclopedia of Great Wizards*. The book took up most of the surface of the table where they sat, and when they asked it to tell them about Iszarre, it groaned as it struggled to lift its own cover. The flipping pages caused a breeze to blow through the library.

A deep, friendly voice said:

> *Iszarre is 676 years old, although he tells people that he is 426 years old. He has spent over 150 years in the Antikrom Mountains where time goes in reverse, and age drops quickly. So, even though he is 676, he doesn't look a day over 357.*
>
> *Iszarre was born on the Day of the Single Moon when Elestra's fifteenth moon was the only moon to rise above the horizon for the entire day. He was the only child born in Elestra that day, and he absorbed all of the magic that would normally be spread out among all newborn babies.*
>
> *The Day of the Single Moon occurs every 25 to 40 years. It always marks the birth of a powerful wizard. When the fifteenth moon is the only one to rise, the most powerful wizards in Elestra's history are born.*

After the day when Iszarre was born, the next time the fifteenth moon rose alone was 345 years ago. The only other time that this has happened since then was 11 years ago.

Iszarre rose through the magical ranks quickly. He was named the Paramage of Quelladon, a city along the Magian border with the Dragon Realms, when he was only 34 years old.

Quelladon was the location of the key fortress during the Stone Dragon Uprising. Iszarre led magical forces from Magia and the Dragon Realms against an army of dragons made of stone from the world of Imbarrion through the fifth moongate.

After his success at Quelladon, Iszarre was put in charge of the magical armies loyal to King Darpasian in the last Magical Tournament 500 years ago. In the final battle, Iszarre faced the dark wizard Blorch and defeated him with a new type of spell that he has never explained to anyone.

Iszarre spent the next twenty years traveling through Elestra and studying prophecies in the most secret of Archives. After returning, King Darpasian named Iszarre Paramage of Amemnop, the most important magical post in all of Elestra.

During his time as Paramage of Amemnop, Iszarre has led the fight against an elusive dark wizard. He has used every bit of magic that he could gather to protect Amemnop after the shield of darkness blocked the light and cut off the magic that flowed into the city from the magical wells throughout Elestra.

The book heaved its cover closed with a mighty grunt. When the dust settled, the book was snoring.

Deanna asked the book fairies to take it back to its shelf. A swarm of nearly twenty tiny fairies looped magical threads around the huge book and dragged it up to its resting place.

Derek looked at the other book, wondering what it would tell them. The book's title was *Magical Chefs of Elestra.* "Okay, tell me what you know about Iszarre," Derek said to the book.

The book flew open, and an excited voice began:

Iszarre, the great wizard, is also Iszarre, the great chef. But, it was not always that way. Here is the story of how he became a chef.

During the Siege of Prellee, when Iszarre defended the city against the invading Cheetahn warlord Ozimel, the food supply ran low. Iszarre developed magical spells to conjure up food for the citizens until the invaders were finally turned back.

He continued to use magical spells to create food for the people he protected, but he realized that he wanted to actually learn to cook. He traveled to Oceania where he studied at the Undersea Academy of Culinary Arts with Master Chef Flot, who is a master of cooking magic into food.

After leaving the Academy, Iszarre cooked at several restaurants in Amemnop and searched for new ingredients with mixed results. He occasionally turned his customers into fish or beetles or caused explosions with his famous Magian Hot Pot.

He eventually decided to focus his culinary exploration on ingredients and dishes from the outworlds. He currently cooks at Glabber's Grub Hut in Amemnop where he offers a variety of Magian, Oceanian, and outworld dishes.

As one reviewer said, Iszarre is magic in the kitchen.

"Oh man," Tobungus said. "We have to order a Hot Pot sometime. I remember once when a group of my friends from back home visited, and we ordered a Hot Pot. It shot soup through the roof."

"Yeah, that sounds great," Deanna said. "We'll have time for explosive food later."

"I wouldn't mind having one of those Hot Pots as a weapon against Eldrack," Derek joked.

"Well, what should we look up next?" Deanna asked.

"How about Glabber?" Derek suggested.

"Sounds good," Deanna said. Turning toward the librarian's desk, she called out, "We're done with this book, and we need to see books that would mention the snake wizard Glabber."

"A book fairy zipped down and took the book from their table back to its shelf. Across the room, a group of fairies was trying to get the huge encyclopedia back off of the shelf, but it wouldn't wake up, so they decided to leave it alone. Instead, they brought a small stack of books that swayed on the thick wooden table.

Glabber

Deanna flicked the wand toward the stack of books and said, "*Explanatum.*" She picked up a book called *Magic in the Desert*. It wasn't nearly as large as the encyclopedia that had told them about Iszarre, but it looked like a good place to start.

"Okay," Deanna said, "Let's hear what you know about Glabber."

The book's cover opened slowly, almost dramatically. The pages fluttered like an ancient hand was trying to remember which page to choose. Finally, after reaching page 113, a voice, somewhere between a whisper and a hiss, said:

> *Glabber slithered his way into the Desert Realm's history books when he stopped the famous sandstorm known as the Wall of Sand.*

A quake just above the Ruby Core caused a massive release of magical energy through the wells of Elestra. The waves of magic circled the world and finally met up, making one giant wave of magical energy along the border between Magia and the Desert Realm.

The magical wave lifted the sands of the Pohorran Desert and created a sandstorm that threatened to engulf much of the Roparcia region of the Desert Realm.

Glabber raced to face the sandstorm and conjured a whirling cyclone of fire to melt the sand into a towering glass mountain. In the years since, carvers have turned the glass mountain into a vertical city that attracts visitors from all over Elestra. The Roparcian Academy of Magic is on the top level of the Glass Mountain.

In honor of his work, Glabber was named Paramage of Roparcia. His years as Paramage were peaceful and were seen as a Golden Age for the Desert Realm. Those days of happiness were shattered on the Day of Darkness when the battle against Eldrack crossed into the Desert Realm.

Shortly after Eldrack's appearance and the disappearance of two of the dark wizard's opponents who were last seen in Roparcia, Glabber left his post as Paramage and went to Magia to join his friend Iszarre as protectors of Amemnop.

"Wow," Deanna said. "Glabber is a lot more powerful than I imagined."

"Oh, yes," Tobungus said. "Iszarre made sure to ask only the strongest wizards to join him in his work."

"I don't understand something," Derek said. "If there are powerful wizards all over Elestra, why doesn't Iszarre gather them all together and go after Eldrack?"

"Some things are not entirely clear," Tobungus replied. "It seems that there is much hidden information in the prophecies, and maybe Iszarre wants to keep this information among a small group of powerful wizards. If Eldrack knows how to defeat an entire army of wizards, then there wouldn't be any defenses left to stop him."

"Alright, I get that," Derek said. "But, it still seems that Iszarre could have more than just Glabber helping him."

"Oh, I think that Iszarre may have more allies than you think," Tobungus explained. "Iszarre once said that his strongest ally would not be known to the enemy until the final battle."

"Hmm, if he has an ally who is more powerful than Glabber, that's good news," Deanna said.

"Let's check the other books about Glabber," Derek said. "Maybe we can learn something else."

The next book on the stack was titled *Odd Facts of the Wizards of Elestra.*

Deanna placed the book in front of her and said, "Can you tell me anything about Glabber?"

The book opened up to page 137, and a grandfatherly voice said:

> *Glabber gained a reputation as the strongest wizard in the Desert Realm after stopping the Wall of Sand. He was summoned to Amemnop by the Great Wizard Iszarre to discuss the major magical problems in the land, but was distracted by tasting butter for the first time.*

Glabber was heard saying that he had never tasted anything so wonderful in all of the magical realms and vowed to eat as much butter as he could before he returned to the Desert Realm.

He ate so much that he began to sweat butter. He became so slippery that he could not slither out of the diner where the two wizards were meeting. He decided that he liked the diner and the butter he ate there so much that he bought it and changed the name to Glabber's Grub Hut.

Since Iszarre was also a famous chef, he accepted Glabber's invitation to run his kitchen, and the two have used the diner as their magical headquarters.

The book closed, so Deanna picked up the next book, titled *The Magic of Elestran Snakes.* "This one looks promising," she said. Turning to the book, she said, "Tell me about Glabber."

The book's cover barely opened. It looked afraid of the information it contained. Finally, a soft voice whispered:

Glabber is from a family of powerful wizards. His father was the Desert Realm's Ambassador to King Barado's Court, but decided that the King's world was too cold. After returning to the Desert Realm, he focused on teaching his sons the magical arts.

Glabber is a Pohorran Sand Viper, so he is strong in hot spells, fire shield defensive magic, wind-based magic, time-slowing spells.

Members of his species are weak against cold magic, ice traps, and dragonic magic.

Glabber has worked with other snake wizards at the Roparcian Academy of Magic in the Glass Mountain on spells that can conjure physical defensive items to protect against cold spells.

I'm sorry, but I really don't like snakes. Just telling you this information gives me the willies.

The book's cover closed slowly, telling the twins that it had told them all it could about Glabber. The book fairies quickly swooped in and returned the books to their shelves.

Eldrack

Deanna and Derek walked over to the fairy librarian's desk to ask for their next set of books. Tobungus said that he wanted to stay at the table and put his shoes in order in his shoe bag.

"Ah, you're back," the librarian said as they approached her desk.

"Yes, we would like books that discuss Eldrack's background," Deanna said. "We want to know where he came from, what sorts of magic he has mastered, that sort of thing."

The librarian paused, looking at them over her tiny glasses. Then she looked toward the towering shelves and repeated Deanna's request.

Derek and Deanna had expected a shower of sparks and the titles of dozens of books to glow, showing the book fairies which books to retrieve, but nothing happened.

"I don't understand," Derek said.

"Let me see if I can help you," the librarian said. We will need the *Elestran Encyclopedia of Great Wizards*."

"Good luck waking that book up," Deanna said.

The librarian chuckled and said, "I'll do it myself." She flew up to the massive book and brought it to their table. She waved her wand over the book's cover and said, "Wake and reveal."

The book shuddered and said, "I'm up. I'm up. What can I do for you?"

"These two young wizards would like to know about Eldrack's background, specifically where he is from and what types of magic he prefers. Any information that describes him would be helpful," the librarian said.

"I have no information of that sort," the book mumbled nervously.

"Eldrack is one of the most powerful wizards in Elestran history," Derek said. "There must be something in there about him."

The book shuddered again. Its cover opened and slammed on the table. The pages flipped quickly from front to back. A wind whipped up from the table toward the shelves lining the walls.

A book on a lower shelf started to shudder, and then another one followed. Soon, all of the books in the library were quaking on their shelves. The sound of the books was like an eerie groan falling from the highest shelves down onto the main floor.

"Did you hear that?" Derek asked.

"Yeah, it sounded like the whole library groaned," Deanna said.

"No, not that," Derek said. "Something called my name."

"I didn't hear anything like that," Deanna replied. She looked over to the librarian to see if she could add anything.

"There are many voices in the library," the fairy librarian explained mysteriously. "Some can only be heard by wizards with certain powers."

"But I don't have any powers that Deanna doesn't have," Derek said.

"Young man," the librarian said, "there are many types of magic, and you may indeed have many powers that your sister does not."

Deanna was still thinking about the books not having information about Eldrack. She looked nervously at the librarian and asked, "Why wouldn't any of the books mention Eldrack?"

The librarian took a deep breath and replied softly, "Everything about Eldrack's past was deleted from the books a long time ago. It scares them, the books, that is."

"Who would do that?" Derek asked in surprise.

The librarian shook her head. "I do not know. It happened well before I came to work here."

"It must have been Eldrack," Deanna said. "He didn't want anyone finding out any information that would help them defeat him."

"That's probably it," Derek agreed. He looked over at Tobungus who was no longer rooting around in his shoe bag. He was looking at the shuddering books with a strange, unreadable look on his face.

Preview of Book 2

Derek and Deanna embark on their second adventure in *The Giants of the Baroka Valley* which is available now. The twins must travel outside of Amemnop to the Baroka Valley where everything is huge, except for one pesky forest elf whose arrogance is as massive as a chicken that happens to be in the right place at the right time.

Of course, Tobungus is along for the ride (on a gong down a boiling river), and they meet a new friend who has an interesting relationship with the mushroom man.

The first chapter begins on the next page, and the story ends in the pages of *The Giants of the Baroka Valley*.

1 Were We Dreaming?

Derek Hughes yawned and stretched in his bed. He had just had the most amazing dream. He closed his eyes to remember the details. In the dream, he and his twin sister Deanna had traveled to a magical land called Elestra where they battled an evil wizard named Eldrack. Their grandfather was captured by Eldrack, but he managed to tell them that they were members of a magical family of Mystical Guardians who protected Elestra. They had recovered the first of fifteen moonstones and were preparing to go off in search of the second. They had spent the previous day at a huge library reading about Elestra and its fifteen moons which acted as gateways to other worlds.

He looked over at the other bed and saw Deanna just starting to stir from a deep sleep. He couldn't wait for her to wake up. He wanted to tell her everything about his dream. "Deanna," he said. "Wake up. I've got to tell you about the most incredible dream."

"Huh?" Deanna mumbled. "Mmmmm," was all she could say.

Derek decided to open the curtains and let the sun wake her up. He walked over to the window and threw the curtains aside. He looked out and froze.

"I'm up, I'm up," Deanna sputtered as the sunlight shot into her eyes. She rubbed her blue eyes and looked at Derek. "What's wrong?" she asked.

"I wanted to tell you about a dream I had," Derek began. "It was the most unbelievable thing ever." He stopped for a few seconds.

"I had a great dream too," Deanna added, as she reached onto her nightstand and grabbed her silver braided headband and put it into her long brown hair. Her grandfather had given her the headband, which was decorated with silver moon-shaped beads, for her eleventh birthday. "We went to this really weird place called Elestra and met the oddest mushroom man." She could see that he was barely listening to her. "Derek!" she blurted out.

"Yeah, yeah, Tobungus, the mushroom man," he mumbled. He turned to her, and she saw that his face was white. "I don't think we were dreaming."

"What?" Deanna whispered. She struggled from under her blankets, jumped out of bed, and ran to the window.

Outside, she saw a bustling crowd moving about the once dusty streets of Amemnop. "Then we really are in Elestra," she murmured.

Memories of the past two days flooded back into her mind. They had started the Fountain of the Six Kingdoms two days earlier and lifted the Spell of Darkness that Eldrack had cast upon the city. Now, Amemnop was becoming the City of Light again, as it was known in its earlier days. It had always been the capital of Magia, the magical kingdom in Elestra, but now people began to enjoy their lives again.

She recalled meeting Iszarre the Great Wizard who worked as a cook at Glabber's Grub Hut. After they found the first moonstone, he told them that he had to visit King Barado to update him on their progress. Before he left, he had told them to look up the Baroka Valley to learn more about their next adventure.

Deanna turned from the window, pulled a purple shirt and jeans from the closet, and quickly got dressed. She loaded up her backpack and made sure to include an extra change of clothes.

Before Derek put his clothes in his backpack, she asked, "Do you want me to change the color of your shirt? Iszarre told me we could do that, and I found the spell in the Book of Spells."

The Book of Spells was contained inside a small book-shaped locket. Their grandfather had given them the locket and the powerful Wand of Ondarell in the Cave of Imprisonment. When the locket was opened, the large, tattered Book of Spells appeared.

"No," Derek began, "I'll just keep the shirt green for now."

Derek wrapped his rope wristband with moon-shaped granite stones around his left wrist and ran a comb through his blond hair. "Don't you think it's time for a haircut?" Deanna teased.

"What? It's not even to my shoulders yet," Derek answered. He checked to make sure that they had everything that they would need for the day. They went downstairs into the diner and had huge stacks of pancakes and strawberries.

They were nearly finished eating when they heard a strange 'clop, clop, clop' sound. When they turned, they saw their friend Tobungus, the mushroom man, walking toward them in a pair of Dutch wooden shoes.

Tobungus was a little over four feet tall, with stubby arms poking out of his mushroom stem body. He had a collection of outlandish shoes to match his bizarre behavior.

"Tobungus," Derek said, "why in the world are you wearing those ridiculous shoes?"

"You have no sense of style, Goober," Tobungus answered. "These shoes may not be comfortable, but they make a great noise when I walk on the wooden sidewalks outside. It's like they're yelling to all of Amemnop that Tobungus is coming."

"My name is Derek! Is that really so hard?" Tobungus was always forgetting their names. This was a common trait for mushroom people, but the names that Tobungus chose to call them were usually ridiculous.

Tobungus waved off Derek's remark and looked at their plates. "Panpies. I love panpies."

"Pancakes," Deanna corrected. "When have you had pancakes?"

"Glabber makes all sorts of stuff from your world. He thinks it makes him exotic." Glabber was the snake wizard who worked with Iszarre in the diner and helped to guard against Eldrack's plans to conquer Elestra.

"Well, we can't sit and talk about food all day," said Deanna, anxious for their next adventure to begin. "We have to get back to the library."

Tobungus closed his shoe bag and said, "Yes, yes. Yesterday you said that we might be going to the Baroka Valley. I'll head over to the Goose Lot and arrange for transport."

"The Goose Lot?" Derek repeated.

"Sure, geese are the fastest way to get most places in Elestra. You can meet me there when you're done." Tobungus stood up and clopped his way back into the street.

"Do you suppose he's the weirdest creature in the universe?" Deanna asked.

"No," Derek answered. "I have a feeling that we'll find much weirder creatures here in Elestra."

They left the diner and headed across town to the State Library of Magia where they would ask the magical books questions about the Baroka Valley. After a few minutes of walking, they noticed that many people seemed to be watching them. They were beginning to feel uneasy and picked up their pace toward the library.

Deanna was just about to pull out the Wand of Ondarell when an old woman squawked, "Look there. The tall boy with the blond hair and the girl with the long brown hair. They're the new Mystical Guardians who started the Fountain."

The other people on the street waved and a few came up to thank them. They suddenly felt very safe in Amemnop, and they wondered if they really needed to leave the city before Iszarre returned from his meeting with King Barado.

"If this is a dream, it's not that bad," Derek whispered to Deanna.

"Come on," she said, pulling him away from the growing crowd. They walked for another ten minutes before they came to the fifteen foot doors that led to the most unusual library they had ever visited.

Peekaboo Pepper Books

The line-up of Peekaboo Pepper Books is expanding quickly. We would like to take this opportunity to provide short previews of other upcoming titles in the *Guardians of Elestra* series.

The Giants of the Baroka Valley: Guardians of Elestra #2 (now available)

Deanna and Derek set out on their second adventure in Elestra with Tobungus the mushroom man at their side. Along the way, they meet Zorell, a cat who has a hate/hate relationship with Tobungus, and ride a giant goose to the Baroka Valley. In the land where everything is huge, from the plants and animals to the grains of sand on a beach, they face off against Eldrack, fend off some sickening gong music, and sail down the River of the Dragon's Breath on an unusual boat. In the end, they are left with a new mystery and a plate of panpies (er, pancakes).

The Desert of the Crescent Dunes: Guardians of Elestra #3 (now available)

Derek and Deanna venture outside of Magia for the first time. They find the Desert Realm to be hot and filled with Eldrack's minions. Their new friend Zorell joins them on the trip, much to Tobungus' dismay. It's a good thing he does, because his dancing proves to be a powerful weapon against Eldrack's army of tentacled sand beasts. Fortunately, the Desert Realm isn't without friends. They meet a resourceful girl named Dahlia who feeds them sugary lizard tails and reads prophecies woven in a hidden tapestry. After finding the entrance to a secret desert, they run into a mysterious statue who points out a solution to their problem. To escape from Eldrack's reach and return the moonstone to the arch, they must cross the Great Snort Pit in a boat scarred with bite marks that are frighteningly large.

The Seven Pillars of Tarook: Guardians of Elestra #4
(available July 2011)

Mount Drasius is cold, very cold, unless you're on the side with the flowing lava. For Derek and Deanna, and their travel partners Tobungus and Zorell, the journey is to the cold side of the mountain. They team up with a band of snowball-throwing kangaroos living near a great temple that just might be the hiding place of the fourth moonstone. Eldrack's magic looks strong enough to finally defeat the twins, until a pair of sweaty socks powers up Deanna's magic.

The Eye of the Red Dragon: Guardians of Elestra #5
(available July 2011)

The twins and their friends accompany Iszarre to King Barado's castle for a picnic that ends with Iszarre arguing with a peach tree about giving him a second piece of fruit. Their search for the fifth moonstone starts with a trip to Tobungus' home, the Torallian Forest, so Zorell must meditate to find a happy place, and Tobungus needs to feed his shoes flipper juice to increase his dancing abilities. If Tobungus seems weird, his friend Rorrdoogo and the Mushroom wizard Bohootus are stranger yet.

But, the real action takes place in the Dragon Realm where a young king finds his way, and his color, and an old dragon gets his mojo back. At the end of their adventure, as usual, Derek and Deanna are left with more questions than answers. Who was this friend who betrayed the older dragon, and where did all of the purple dragon wizards go?

The Misty Peaks of Dentarus: Guardians of Elestra #6 (available August 2011)

A trip to the mountains would be a nice way for Derek and Deanna to relax after their first five encounters with Eldrack. Unfortunately, these are the Antikrom Mountains where time occasionally goes in reverse, and where valleys are perfect places for an ambush by Eldrack's forces. The Iron Forest floats above the highest peaks, and the twins learn that sometimes the right jacket is all you need to fly. They meet their uncle the yak farmer who insists that he must stay out of the family's battle against Eldrack. That's too bad because he could tip balance in their favor.

Author Bio

Thom Jones is the author of the *Guardians of Elestra* series, as well as two forthcoming series, *Galactic Gourmets* (science fiction) and *The Adventures of Boron Jones* (superhero meets chemistry).

He has taught subjects including history, atmospheric science, and criminal justice at various colleges. What he loves to do most, though, is work with kids, which he does in crime scene camps that he runs. He began writing the *Guardians of Elestra* stories in 2004 for his two sons. The stories evolved, and Tobungus got stranger over the years. He finally decided to start Peekaboo Pepper Books and publish the stories with the view that kids are smart and funny, and that they are more engaged by somewhat challenging vocabulary and mysteries woven throughout the stories they read.

He lives in the Adirondacks with his wife Linda and their three children, Galen, Aidan, and Dinara. He is extremely lucky to have such wonderful editors in Linda, Galen, and Aidan, who have found too many errors to count and have come up with fantastic ideas, even when they don't know it.

8791843R0

Made in the USA
Charleston, SC
15 July 2011